I left Zoey at a   ne had
thoughtfully grab.... ... a meal. She was the
bride, after all.

Everyone had their food and was back in their
places on the picnic benches. The conversation
had quieted as people focused on their lobsters. I
worked my way through the crowd, showing someone how to use the nutcracker on their lobster's
claws, tying on another person's bib, answering
questions about the meal and the history of the island. Servers ran to and fro with more water and
iced tea, and there was regular, but not overwhelming business at the bar.

All seemed to be going well when I heard a loud
thump and saw several of the people at Jamie's
parents' table jump up. The man in the blue
blazer had fallen backward off his bench.

"He's allergic!" a woman screamed. I didn't see
who.

The man lay on the deck of the dining pavilion,
gasping for air. I ran toward him, cursing under my
breath. He was bright red, clutching his throat. My
heart raced, fearing what could be happening . . .

Books by Barbara Ross

Maine Clambake Mysteries
Clammed Up
Boiled Over
Musseled Out
Fogged Inn
Iced Under
Stowed Away
Steamed Open
Sealed Off
Shucked Apart
Muddled Through
Hidden Beneath
Torn Asunder

Collections
Egg Nog Murder
(with Leslie Meier and Lee Hollis)
Yule Log Murder
(with Leslie Meier and Lee Hollis)
Haunted House Murder
(with Leslie Meier and Lee Hollis)
Halloween Party Murder
(with Leslie Meier and Lee Hollis)
Irish Coffee Murder
(with Leslie Meier and Lee Hollis)
Easter Basket Murder
(with Leslie Meier and Lee Hollis)

Jane Darrowfield Mysteries
Jane Darrowfield, Professional Busybody
Jane Darrowfield and the Madwoman Next Door

Published by Kensington Publishing Corp.

TORN ASUNDER

Barbara Ross

Kensington Publishing Corp.
www.kensingtonbooks.com

This book is dedicated to Luke Donius, extraordinary husband and father, professional scientist, and amateur gardener. You are the best son-in-law we ever could have wished for.

CHAPTER ONE

I walked my friends Zoey Butterfield and Jamie Dawes through the first-floor function rooms of Windsholme, the mansion built by my mother's ancestors on Morrow Island. My stomach fluttered with equal parts excitement and anxiety. I cared so much what they thought.

In the old main salon, the round tables and accompanying chairs were set out, seating for one hundred of Zoey and Jamie's nearest and dearest. Fourteen crisply ironed white tablecloths sat on a sideboard, ready to be put into service. Another sideboard held the salad, dinner, and dessert plates lovingly designed and handmade by Zoey, on which we'd serve the wedding feast. The day was beautiful, not always a given in early June in coastal Maine. The sun shone through the French doors, bathing the enormous room in a rosy, nuptial glow.

Zoey sighed. "It's perfect."

I nodded enthusiastically, hoping my smile looked affirming. In truth, I would have been happier if this wedding, in which I was doing triple duty as the maid of honor, wedding planner, and venue manager, had come later in the season, after we'd had a chance to work out some kinks. Zoey was my closest friend, as well as my boss and business partner at Lupine Design, her ceramics company. Jamie had been a neighbor and good friend since our kindergarten days waiting for the yellow school bus that took us to Busman's Harbor Elementary. I loved him like a brother and wanted only the best for him.

I cared about every wedding we would hold this summer in our newly renovated space. But for those other events, I was working with a team of people related to or hired by the happy couple. For this wedding, I was the team.

When they'd announced their engagement the previous summer, Zoey and Jamie said they would hold their wedding on any summer weekend we had available. Then, this spring, there'd been a sudden flurry of news and activity. The bride's former teacher, who was to be the officiant, was going to be in Europe and was only available in June. Jamie's elderly parents weren't getting any younger. Et cetera. Et cetera. As a result of all this, he and Zoey ended up grabbing the first weekend in June, the first wedding we'd host. I'd barely gotten the staff hired for the traditional Maine clambakes we ran on the island from Father's Day through Columbus Day. The last summer employee, a server, had signed on three days before. Thank goodness, he'd been available immediately.

"Let's keep going," I said. "The rehearsal's in two hours, and we still need to get dressed." I led them through the big oval foyer, where the ceremony would take place. The three of us inspected the winding grand staircase. Zoey ran her fingers along the banister, as if she was imagining herself floating down the steps in her flowing white gown. Jamie looked stunned, like he couldn't believe the day was nearly upon us.

I was happy that, when they gazed upward, they didn't see what I did: a man hanging from the stair rail, the best man at the last wedding we'd held on the island seven years earlier. It was his murder, and the fire that had consumed the derelict mansion in its aftermath, that had forced the decision about what to do with the house and resulted in its subsequent renovation. I shuddered, pushing all thoughts of those awful days firmly out of my mind, and turned back to look at Jamie and Zoey. Their wedding would be a fresh start, chasing the ghosts away.

They were an attractive couple. I'd always thought so. Jamie was tall and well-built with bright blue eyes, dark brows and lashes, and the kind of tannable skin that shouldn't have come with his blond hair.

Zoey's brown curls were loose for the party tonight. I was used to seeing them tied up with a bandanna as she worked in the pottery studio. She was curvy and sturdy, of the earth, with large features, including an oversized mouth. She shouldn't have been pretty—and wasn't, if you looked at each of her features individually. But, when they were taken in combination, in a face that was constantly in motion—curious, surprised, fascinated, determined—she was beautiful.

We passed through to the mansion's original dining room. "We'll have breakfast here in the morning for the wedding party," I said. "Then we'll take

the table to the main salon to use as the head table
for the wedding reception. The pocket doors between the dining room and the grand foyer will be
opened to make more room for people to stand
during the ceremony and for dancing."

I glanced at Zoey as she took it all in. I'd been
surprised, more than surprised, by her strong desire for a highly traditional wedding. She had no
living relatives. Her mother had never married,
and Zoey had never met her father. She was an
artist, a brilliant potter. Her friends were scattered
across the country in the places where she'd
honed her skills and learned the business. Close as
we were, she and I had never shared wedding fan-
tasies until hers was happening. At first, I'd
thought Zoey's drive for the white gown, the head
table, the formal meal, had been to please Jamie's
family. Later, I understood it came from somewhere inside her. Maybe it was a desire to live a life
different from her mother's. Maybe the white wedding was something she'd dreamed of as a child,
seeing the photos of her friends' parents' weddings when she stayed over, invited by their sympathetic mothers during bad days of her childhood.
Those photos had probably meant stability and
safety to her.

The wedding rehearsal would be at four o'clock.
The rehearsal dinner, with fifty or so out-of-town
and special guests invited, was this evening. It
would be a traditional Snowden Family Clambake
meal: twin lobsters, the softshell clams called steamers, an ear of corn, a potato, an onion and an egg
cooked over a wood fire, covered by seaweed and
saltwater-soaked tarps. In deference to the bride's
gown and the guests' good clothes, the wedding

meal tomorrow would be more sedate, easier-to-consume lobster tails, beef, or vegan entrées.

We toured the upstairs guest rooms. The bulk of tonight's guests would leave the island on the *Jacquie II*, the tour boat that brought our customers to Morrow Island. Then they, along with fifty or so additional guests, would arrive again the next afternoon in the same way for the wedding. The members of the wedding party would be staying overnight with us to be on hand for photos the next day. Windsholme wasn't an inn and wasn't licensed as such. Those who stayed would be our guests. During the renovation, our architect and general contractor had persuaded us to provide walls, plumbing, and electricity for a bath for every room as a hedge against future need. We'd been finishing the bathrooms as time and finances allowed.

Zoey looked into every bedroom designated for the wedding party. "All good," she pronounced when we reached the last one. Jamie nodded his agreement, although I thought he was less interested in the flowers and chocolates provided for each guest than in how well-stocked the bar downstairs would be. He seemed happy with his last bachelor quarters, a series of three connected rooms that ran along the front of the second floor, ready for him, his best man, and his single groomsman.

"Do you want to see your room?" I asked Zoey.

"My room? Aren't I staying with you?"

"Of course, if you want to." Zoey had spent many nights on Morrow Island, always staying with me in my apartment at the end of the hall. Fashioned out of the old nursery, the living space ran the length of the house, with views of the water on three sides. There was a single bedroom and a bath as well. "I thought you might want your own space."

"To fret and be nervous in?" she responded, "I don't think so."

"Good," I said. "Done. Shall we go down?"

I put a hand over my eyes to shield them from the sun as the three of us came out onto the big front porch that spanned the façade of Windsholme. A cool breeze blew off the water. The information Zoey had meticulously assembled warned tonight's guests to bring shawls and sweaters. I hoped they'd take heed.

"They're here," Jamie said, calm as you please. He pointed to the water, where my brother-in-law, Sonny, steered our Boston Whaler toward the dock. We ran down Windsholme's great lawn to help with the boat and greet the first arrivals. By arrangement, this first boatload held staff.

Sonny was in charge of the fire that would cook the Clambake meal. With him were his two assistants. Fortunately, both men had worked at the Clambake the previous summer and knew how to get started without him. Sonny would return to the town pier immediately to pick up the rest of the wedding party for the rehearsal.

My sister, Livvie, was also on the early boat with her cooks. Livvie oversaw the parts of the Clambake meal that came out of our small kitchen: the clam chowder that was the first course, the heated clam juice for dredging the steamers, the melted butter for dipping the lobster meat, and the blueberry grunt, swimming in vanilla ice cream, that we served for dessert. The cooks were also in charge of prepping the food for the wood fire, washing the potatoes, peeling the onions, and shucking the corn during late summer when it was fresh. This time of year, the ears were frozen, and therefore had been pre-shucked, making the job a tiny bit easier. Livvie's two cooks had been with us for years. As they walked toward the kitchen, Livvie gave me a wave and hurried behind them. "Gotta get going so I'm on time for the rehearsal!" Livvie was the other attendant for Zoey.

The other passengers were the caterers. So far, we had booked only weekend events at Windsholme, so I hadn't hired any permanent staff. Instead, I'd given each bride and groom a list of suggested caterers. I was thrilled when, after their tasting, Jamie and Zoey had chosen Carol Trevett. She was experienced and professional, and I knew her. She'd come out in advance to inspect Windsholme's new kitchen and pronounced it "excellent," which made me unexpectedly blush with pride. I was more invested in the renovation being successful than I'd thought.

Carol had brought two assistants, both middle-aged women. One was tall and thin, dark-haired, with intense blue eyes. Carol introduced her as Mel. The other was short and round. Cassie Howard. I knew her from around town.

Finally, last off the boat was Jordan Thomas, the Snowden Family Clambake's newest hire. He had a gym bag with him, presumably filled with night things and fresh clothes, because he'd agreed to take on some extra duties this afternoon and then to stay over and serve breakfast to the wedding party in the morning. He was nineteen, a lanky kid with a flop of sandy-blond hair, wide brown eyes, and a face that would be boyish when he was fifty. I would have preferred to use one of our experienced staff, but Jordan had both restaurant and banquet experience. When I'd emailed his references in California, they'd been effusive in their praise and said they were sorry to lose him.

With the caterers came big plastic containers of food and ingredients, some for the hors d'oeuvres they'd serve during the cocktail hour this evening and some for the feast tomorrow. Carol had also agreed to prepare the vegan entrée chosen by some of tonight's guests in lieu of the clambake. We always offered chicken or hot dogs for non-lobster-eating customers, but Zoey had insisted there would be demand for a vegan alternative, and she wasn't wrong.

Jamie, Zoey, and I pitched in to fetch and carry.

After we'd delivered the food to Windsholme's kitchen, my brother-in-law, Sonny, and I huddled as the others went about their business.

"Have you been watching this storm?" His bright red eyebrows beetled together.

"Yes." *How could I not?* At the Snowden Family Clambake Company, we always kept an eye on the weather. More than half our picnic tables were outside. This storm, originally a Spring hurricane, had long since been downgraded to a tropical storm and then to whatever came after that. Perhaps just a storm. Nevertheless, since it was once a hurricane and therefore had a name, its journey up the East Coast had been breathlessly reported.

Currently, the storm was predicted to flash through our area overnight, bringing strong winds, high seas, heavy rain, and maybe even a bit of unusual June thunder and lightning.

"I'm hoping we can thread the needle tonight," I told Sonny. "We'll get everyone back on board the *Jacquie II* before it starts. The storm is supposed to end before dawn, so we'll have time for any cleanup in the morning. Everyone arrives back for the wedding at two tomorrow afternoon, so no problem." I sounded more confident than I felt.

Sonny drew his lips in, looking unconvinced. He'd recently shaved off his winter beard, and the skin on his chin beneath the freckles on his cheeks was whiter than white. I didn't blame him for the skeptical look, nor did I doubt the cause of it. Forecasts were fine, but unfortunately Mother Nature never listened to them.

"Do they know?" He jerked his head toward Jamie and Zoey, now back on Windsholme's front porch, holding hands and talking.

"I'm sure Jamie does," I said. "Probably Zoey, too, but she's deliberately ignoring it. Too many other things on her mind."

"Any chance we can move the whole shindig up?"

I thought about it for a moment, not for the first time, but the complications of somehow reaching the fifty invited guests and telling them to be at the town pier earlier than planned seemed impossible to conquer. "We'll stay the course," I said.

Sonny nodded. He knew how difficult it would be to make the change as well as I did. "Okay. We all staffed up?"

"We're okay for tonight and tomorrow. I got our regulars back for the occasion." Our jobs were popular with teachers and students, including several who were local. They were hard to schedule in June, as the school year wound to a close with proms, sports banquets, and the like. Luckily, there was nothing on tonight, so we'd have experienced staff.

"We have one completely green waiter," I told him.

"Jordan," Sonny said. "I met him on the boat ride over." Sonny knew all the staff, even at this early point in the year. "Seems like a good kid."

"Yes. I needed a server at Windsholme this afternoon, and no one else was available." The teachers and students had school. The others were either finishing up winter jobs or attending to part-time work they'd keep through the Clambake season.

"It'll be fine." He put his big paw on my shoulder, patted once, and then walked down to the firepit to check on his guys. Immediately after that, he'd take the Whaler back to town.

In addition to the wedding party and Jamie's parents, the next trip would include Jack and Page, Livvie and Sonny's kids, and my mom, who ran the Snowden Family Clambake gift shop. There wouldn't be any call for the gift shop tonight. Zoey had asked Mom to come early and attend the rehearsal.

Neither Mom nor Sonny and Livvie had moved out to live on the island yet. Livvie's kids were still in school, Jack in first grade and Page, impossible for my brain to grasp, a junior in high school. Like the other New England states, public school in Maine finished at the very end of June, so Livvie's family remained at their split-level house up the peninsula from Busman's Harbor.

Mom had no reason not to move out to her apartment in Windsholme at the opposite end of the hallway from mine, except that the weather in early June was still highly changeable. And, her fiancé, George, the captain of our tour boat, was based in town.

Le Roi, the Maine Coon cat who lived with Mom and me at the house in the harbor where I'd grown up, also hadn't yet moved out to Windsholme. Le Roi loved the island. What cat wouldn't? No cars or predators and an endless supply of softhearted guests to sneak him bits of lobster and clams under their tables. I wished I'd had Le Roi for company while I was alone on Morrow Island. But on balance, I'd decided he'd be nothing but a pain in the rear at our first wedding of the season in a house full of people bringing temptations like bridal gowns and flower arrangements. So he'd stayed in town.

I saw Sonny off and returned to Windsholme. I found Jordan in the kitchen, talking with the caterers. "Welcome aboard," I greeted him. "Come with me. Do you know how to open a bottle of champagne?"

CHAPTER TWO

Every eye in the room was on Zoey as she walked down Windsholme's grand staircase in time to the guitar music playing softly below. She wore a goofy grin, no doubt in part because she was carrying a paper plate covered with the bows from the gifts she'd received at her very traditional bridal shower. Livvie, clearly more aware of her duties as an attendant than I, had made Zoey a veil from a particularly gaudy shower curtain.

After reviewing the order of the ceremony and bossing everyone into place in my role as wedding planner, I had stepped to the front of the room and stood, waiting, in my role as the maid of honor.

From the bottom of the stairs, Jamie watched his intended with open-mouthed joy.

I glanced across at my mom. Her delicate brows were pulled together in consternation. "I would have walked her down," Mom mouthed at me, evidently not happy with the idea of Zoey walking alone.

"It's what she wants," I mouthed back. This was one piece of tradition Zoey had let go. She would walk down the stairs alone. No one would "give her away." She would look dramatic and spectacular in her real gown, not the short, pale pink dress she currently wore, which showed off her sturdy but shapely legs. Zoey was alone, without a mother or father. She was her own self, to do with as she pleased.

At the bottom of the staircase, Jamie took Zoey's arm and led her to the front of the room, where the officiant awaited, along with the assembled wedding party: me, Livvie, and Pete Howland, the best man and Jamie's partner on the Busman's Harbor police force. The other groomsman, Jamie's nephew, was absent. He hadn't shown up in time to catch the Whaler, though Sonny had waited as long as he could. By text, the errant groomsman had been told to come out on the tour boat with the rest of the guests.

The bride and groom arrived at the designated spot and turned to each other. The guitarist strummed to a stop. He was Bill Lascelle, a former mentor of Zoey's. She'd worked in his ceramics studio. He looked to be in his early fifties and had white hairs blooming in the black curls at his temples. He played the guitar beautifully.

Everyone looked at the officiant expectantly. Her hair was long and gray, pulled back in a simple, low ponytail. She wore a purple-gray dress that hung loosely from her small body "Call me Constance," she had said when we'd been introduced earlier, taking both my hands in hers.

"Dearly beloved," she began. "We are gathered here . . ."

I stole a glance at the other two people in the room, Jamie's parents. Jamie had come along very late in their lives, ten years after his nearest sibling. "The exclamation point at the end of the sentence," his mother said.

"Yes." Jamie's dad always agreed. "The sentence was 'Surprise!'"

They were more than twenty years older than my mother, and I was a little nervous about how they'd react to Constance Marshall, who clearly hadn't been ordained by any authority greater than the World Wide Web. But, as Jamie had assured me, his parents had been to enough weddings of nieces, nephews, grandchildren, children of their friends, and friends of their children not to be surprised by anything. Both of them beamed at their youngest child, who stood straight, trying not to act flustered. When Mr. Dawes caught me looking at him, he mouthed, "I would have walked her down."

I smiled and shook my head, and he smiled back.

By prior arrangement, the bride and groom didn't read their vows, wanting them to be a surprise for all of us. Constance Marshall called for the rings, and Pete pantomimed not finding them, patting each of his pockets at an increasingly furious pace. Everyone laughed, and the tension went out of the room.

Constance finished up quickly. "By the power granted to me by the State of Maine, I pronounce you husband and wife. What God has joined together, let no one tear asunder. You may kiss."

Blushing deeply, Jamie leaned forward and pecked Zoey on the mouth. I'd seen them make out with more vigor in my kitchen. The guitar started up again, and Jordan, the new waiter, appeared through the door from the dining room with a tray of filled champagne flutes. We each took one and toasted the happy couple. "To the bride and groom!" Mr. Dawes cried.

Livvie and I took one sip each and set down our glasses. We'd be working hard this evening. Zoey didn't touch her drink. I thought she must have been planning for a long night. "Now for the party!" she yelled.

Jordan and I cleaned the champagne flutes in the kitchen, which was momentarily quiet as the caterers readied the high-top tables for the cocktail party on the great lawn nearest Windsholme. Jordan hand-washed the delicate glasses as I dried.

"What brought you to Busman's Harbor?" I should have asked that during his job interview. The answer might have given me a sense of whether I could count on him to stay for the whole summer. Had Jordan moved to Busman's Harbor to live, or was he a backpacker who'd take off as soon as he had whatever he judged to be enough money?

"I moved here with my mom," he answered. He looked like he was going to say more, but he didn't.

"Your mom's here, too?" I'd imagined he was on his own.

"Yes. She, um . . ." He searched for the right word, or the courage to tell the truth, I wasn't sure which. "She finished up with her job at home, and I wasn't in school. She said we could go anywhere in the country, since we were both free. I didn't have any ideas. I never thought of leaving California. But Mom said she'd always wanted to live on the Maine coast, so we came."

Maine seemed like an odd place for him to land, given the number of two-year and four-year colleges and universities in California. "You didn't plan to go to college?"

He shook his head. "I was in college, but I left. I need to earn some money first."

A common-enough story. We continued washing and drying. "When did you arrive in Maine?"

"A month ago."

"Where are you living?" Finding housing during the run-up to tourist season in a resort town would have been challenging.

He named a campground a ways up the peninsula. It was clean and well-cared-for, but would have been cold and uncomfortable when Jordan and his mother had arrived in early May.

"You packed up and came cross-country," I said. "That was brave. Was it a grand adventure?"

Jordan smiled for the first time since I'd started the conversation. "Sometimes. We saw the Grand Canyon, ranches in Texas with real cowboys. We crossed the Mississippi at Memphis and toured Graceland."

Something in his tone made me ask, "And other times, it wasn't such a grand adventure?"

"It was a big move," he answered. "I've never lived anywhere but LA. I didn't know what we were in for. But Mom really wanted to come, so I did it. For her."

CHAPTER THREE

We went out to the front porch just in time to see the *Jacquie II* pulling up at the dock. The rehearsal dinner guests—dressed casually, as instructed—streamed off in a cloud of chatter that seemed to become even louder as the boat's engines died.

The rest of the wedding party headed down to greet the new arrivals, but Zoey didn't move. I hung back with her, wondering if the real beginning of the wedding weekend was overwhelming for her. I knew Zoey well. She wasn't easily daunted. But she'd imagined this for so long. Could the reality match the dream? She stared at the people coming off the boat as if she'd never seen any of them before.

"You okay?" I asked.

"So okay." She turned to me and smiled, but she still didn't move.

"Constance is going to do a great job," I said, by way of making conversation. *Focus on the little suc-*

cesses of the day, I thought. *Remind her things are going well.*

"I knew she would," Zoey responded. "I wanted her to be here so much. She was my art teacher in high school, the first person who ever saw something in me. She encouraged me to apply to art school for college. She was the only adult who was a constant in my life after my mother died."

"Does she have a partner or a family?" I was intrigued by the woman. She seemed to have an inner calm that I envied.

"I think her students are her family," Zoey said. "I'm not the only one who keeps in touch. She has this marvelous bungalow near Griffith Park. Sometimes she'd invite me after school. It was the only place I could completely relax." Zoey paused. "She retired this year. It must be a big change for her."

It had taken some time for Zoey to open up to me about her difficult childhood and her mother's murder. I knew from experience she didn't want my sympathy. She wanted me to hear her stories and accept them, as any friend talking to another. Parts of her life had been exceptionally sad, but it was also her life. The facts of her life.

Zoey still didn't move, though the boat was half-empty. The guests milled around near the dock, greeting the rest of the wedding party.

"Bill plays the guitar very well," I said, keeping up the conversation.

"I've listened to him so many times," Zoey said. "I worked at his studio in Denver for two years. In the evenings, he'd play, and we'd all sing. Bill taught me a lot about ceramics, but even more about the business."

I made a mental note to be sure to talk to Bill

Lascelle. Now that I was the business manager of
Lupine Design, I would've loved some words of wis-
dom from someone far more experienced than me.

"He took me under his wing," Zoey was saying,
"I'll always be grateful. I want to achieve what he
has."

"Then you will," I said. "But first you're getting
married."

My last remark seemed to move Zoey off the
dime. "Yes, I am," she said, flashing her killer
smile. Then, suddenly, she was bounding down the
lawn toward the dock, waving her arms and shout-
ing, "Welcome!"

"Julia!" Vee Snugg, waving madly, was one of the
last off the boat. She clutched me to her formida-
ble bosom. Vee and her sister, Fee, lived in their B
and B, the Snuggles Inn, across the street from my
mother's house in Busman's Harbor. The sisters
were friends of my mother and late father, and
honorary great-aunts to Livvie and me. When Zoey
came along, they took her naturally into their big
hearts. They had been the hosts of Zoey's bridal
shower and were the only people to whom we hadn't
needed to give the instruction "very traditional"
with regard to Zoey's wishes. They wouldn't have
known how to do things any other way.

Vee was one of the few who hadn't heeded the
directions to dress casually. Or perhaps she had
dressed casually, for her. Her pure-white hair was,
as always, wrestled into a chignon that hadn't
moved despite the breeze on the boat ride over.
She was dressed in a well-cut maroon skirt and a
well-cut pink blouse, and had a white, cotton cardi-

gan over her arm. Hearty Mainer though she was, she'd be glad of that later. She was fully made up, her lips a lively red, and she completed her ensemble with her omnipresent nylon stockings and high heels.

Her sister followed her off the boat. Fee, bent with arthritis, was also in a skirt, but a denim one. Less effusive than her sister, she put a hand on my arm. I put my hand over hers and squeezed.

Next off the boat were my former landlord, Gus, and his wife, Mrs. Gus. Gus still regarded Zoey with some suspicion as a newcomer though she'd eaten breakfast in his restaurant several times a week since I'd first taken her there a year ago. The couple had known Jamie since he was born, and his parents were old friends.

"Lovely evening," Mrs. Gus said, glancing at the still blue sky.

"Let's hope it stays that way," Gus grumped, reminding me about the storm, one of my many worries about tonight's party, albeit one I couldn't do anything about.

I cast a hurried look up the terraced great lawn to the area where our picnic tables stood. The experienced staff were already busy, setting up their serving stations and putting on each picnic table the cutlery, including nutcrackers and picks for the lobsters, the rolls of paper towels that served as napkins, and pitchers of water and iced tea.

Craning my neck slightly, I could see into the dining pavilion, where our bartender was dispensing the stronger stuff. There was a crowd around the bar. I hoped he would be able to keep up.

My boyfriend, Tom, was the last passenger off the *Jacquie II*, after he'd helped any guests in need of assistance onto the gangway. I flew into his arms, so relieved to see him. He was an invited guest, but Maine State Police detectives often got called out on their days off. I was thankful that wasn't the case today.

"Whoa, Julia. Is everything okay?"

"Yes," I answered. "It's just that," I waved my arm around, encompassing the whole island, "it's Zoey's and Jamie's wedding. I want it to be perfect."

He opened his arms, and I stepped back. Still holding my hands, he searched my eyes. "Pre-wedding jitters? On the part of the maid of honor. Is that usual?"

"And the wedding planner, and the venue manager," I said. "And there's a storm coming, and new staff, and the first clambake of the year, first event inside Windsholme, and, and, and . . ."

He squeezed my hand. "Just breathe. It's going to be okay."

As we walked toward the clambake, I breathed in and then out, and unclenched my jaw. I leaned into Tom's chest, under his strong shoulder, where I fit perfectly. He was a handsome man, his body toned by hours in the gym. His features were regular and angular, the planes of his nose and cheeks sharp. His round, heavily lashed brown eyes softened his face. In them, I saw the boy who had become the man.

We'd been together for almost a year. We were headed toward the dining pavilion where we'd had our first kiss, finally admitting to an attraction that had been a long, slow burn. I had been with someone else; then he had been with someone else. He was brokenhearted; then I was. But there was nothing of the rebound in our relationship. He was a smart, steady man, who made me laugh and who supported me in everything I did. Even this. Crazy this.

"I have to check on the bar," I told him.

"I know." He took my hand again and then reluctantly let go as I walked away. He knew what it was to have to go to work, even when you didn't want to. "It will be fine," he called, his voice just loud enough for me to hear.

CHAPTER FOUR

I helped at the bar through the first crush and then excused myself to tend to everything else. When I peeked into the Clambake's small kitchen, Livvie turned from a steaming pot of clam chowder to give me a quick thumbs-up. Sonny similarly waved me away from the Clambake fire. He had everything under control. I answered several questions from the waitstaff. All was fine, so I went to wander among the crowd.

It was easy to tell Zoey's artist friends from Jamie's large, extended family. Originally from Maine, Jamie's parents and siblings now lived in far-flung locations from Florida to Oregon. They'd flown in especially for the wedding and were excited to see one another and to greet the cousins, aunts, and uncles who still lived in town. They clustered in groups, holding drinks and chatting happily. I listened in as I walked through the crowd.

"Just graduated from . . ."

"Engaged to . . ."

"Opened a hair salon in . . ."

"Retired from . . ."

Like most American families, they were spread across income, education, religious, and political divides and embraced an ever-more-diverse gene pool.

I was relieved to see that the groomsman nephew had shown up on the boat. He'd be spending the night at Windsholme, so now that we had a hold of him, we wouldn't let him go. Given the age spread in Jamie's family, he and his nephew, who was named Dan Dawes, were the same age. Dan had grown up in California, but he'd spent his summers with his grandparents, Jamie's parents, in Maine. He and Jamie had been much more like cousins than uncle and nephew, and I remembered Dan coming out to the Clambake as a teenager. I went to greet him, sticking out my hand.

"Dan, I'm Julia Snowden. I don't know if you re-member—"

"Julia! Of course"—he brought me in for a bear hug—"I remember you. And this magical place." He held his arms out straight and turned from side to side, a gesture taking in the whole of Morrow Island. "I have the happiest memories."

He looked remarkably like Jamie. Same height, tannable skin, dark brows, and dark lashes, except that Jamie was blond, and Dan's hair, equally thick, was a dark chestnut brown, slightly long and expensively cut. He was wearing well-designed plaid shorts, a cotton shirt that looked like it had been tailor-made for him, and an oatmeal-colored sweater around his shoulders. Though he was a good-looking man, I realized it was Jamie's un-usual combination of coloring that made him so striking.

I smiled back. I loved it when people appreciated Morrow Island.

"I hear you're back in town, running the Clambake," Dan said.

"And working for Zoey, your soon-to-be aunt."

"Aunt." He laughed and looked over at Zoey, still surrounded by friends.

"What are you doing now?" I asked.

Dan had founded a company that did something related to how animation was generated for movies and games. I'd left my venture-capital job in New York eight years earlier, but I could barely comprehend the torrent of computer acronyms and animation terms that made up Dan's description of his company. He'd sold the business a few years earlier, which brought us to the part of the story I did understand from my previous work. Dan Dawes was rich. Not regular rich. Really rich.

I'd met so many of these rich achievers during my venture-capital days. Any family might have one, the one who didn't just make good, but made it big. I wondered idly who that would be in our family. My money was on my niece, Page.

Dan was investing in new companies now. We talked for a few minutes, trading war stories from my New York days, and then I excused myself to check on how things were going.

Carol Trevett's two assistants were passing hors d'oeuvres, something we didn't offer at the regular clambakes. Usually while guests waited for their meals, they hiked around the island, played volleyball or bocce, or watched Sonny and his crew cook over the wood fire. Jamie and Zoey had guessed that their friends and family, long separated, would want time to chat, so the cocktail party and passed hors d'oeuvres were the solution.

We didn't want people to fill up because the clambake was a big meal. Jamie and Zoey had picked shrimp cocktail, bacon-wrapped scallops, and stuffed mushrooms. The big splurge was lobster-caviar canapés, small puff pastries filled with layers of mushrooms duxelles, lobster meat warmed in butter, crème fraîche, caviar, and chopped chives.

As Cassie Howard, the shorter, rounder server, passed by, I popped one in my mouth and savored it. It was earthy from the mushrooms, briny from the lobster, and rich from the caviar and crème fraîche.

"Fantastic!" I called to Cassie as she kept moving through the crowd. She managed a thumbs-up despite the stack of napkins she carried in her left hand.

Like Jamie's family, Zoey's guests had come from all over the country. Driven to achieve both artistic and commercial success, Zoey had moved from California, where she'd grown up and gone to school, to Michigan, then Texas, then Colorado, where she'd worked with Bill Lascelle, and on to New York City, where she'd started Lupine Design. Finally, she had moved herself and her company to Busman's Harbor, Maine, based on an article she'd read on a tourist website. Her crowd was colorful and loud, and predictably more varied and bohemian than Jamie's family. In addition to Constance and Bill, Zoey had invited former bosses, mentors, fellow art students, colleagues, and collaborators. Many of them knew each other through a web of associations and were happy to be together for the first time in a long time. Their conversations were different from Jamie's family's, but just as excited.

"Won an award for . . ."

"Was shown at a gallery in . . ."

"I'm teaching at . . ."

"So fantastic, I couldn't believe . . ."

Zoey was in a corner on Windsholme's front porch, friends all around her. I approached the group, and she introduced me. "Suki, Stella, Jojo, Montana, Derek, and—"

"Amelia," Derek supplied. He was standing next to Zoey, his arm around her, no daylight between them.

I knew who Derek was. I'd been surprised when Zoey told me she'd invited an ex. "I've told you, I've almost always had amicable breakups, usually because I was moving for work, no harm done." She paused. "This particular ex, Derek Quinn, was my college boyfriend. I owe him a lot, and he's remained a friend."

"Hmm, okay," I'd responded. "Does Jamie know about this invitation?"

"Of course," Zoey had said. "Besides, Derek's bringing a plus-one."

I'd wondered how Jamie felt about this. But he was a lot more sophisticated and tolerant than the small-town cop he appeared to be.

Seeing Derek Quinn, the ex, in the flesh was something else. The proprietary nature of his hover next to Zoey made me uncomfortable. Amelia must be the plus-one. When I looked at her, I had to clamp my mouth shut to keep it from dropping open. Amelia looked uncannily like Zoey. Same long, curly brown hair. Same curvy body, though Amelia was a couple of inches shorter. And about

fifteen years younger. She wasn't as pretty as my
friend, but she had the same big features.

Derek Quinn sure has a type, I thought, looking at
the two women. Surely other people were noticing.

It didn't take a mind reader to see how Amelia
was feeling. Her brows were pulled down in a suspicious squint.

Jamie and Zoey had been aware that their
camps would clump together if left to their own
devices. For tomorrow, for the wedding meal,
they'd taken care of that with place cards, min-
gling the groups together. But, for tonight, the
first night, people would be eager to catch up. The
bride and groom had agreed people should sit
with whomever they pleased.

I could place almost every person I saw into one
of the groups—Dawes family, artist, local—though
there were a few wild cards. One I particularly noticed was an older man, slightly overdressed in a
blue blazer. He was good-looking, with regular features, a full head of white hair, and a dapper mustache. He moved smoothly through the crowd,
talking to Zoey's friends, Jamie's family, and the locals. I could see he had a kind of easy charm. I
wondered who he was and groped for a name on
the seating chart for the next day, a man unat-
tached to any other person or group, but couldn't
remember anyone.

As I watched, Constance Marshall approached
him and started a conversation. Did that mean he
was one of Zoey's friends? As I walked around the
party, I checked back on them several times. They
talked for a few minutes, and then the tone changed.
The man, facing me, responded to Constance with

a look of confusion and then shook his head in denial. Constance had her back to me, her shoulders tight and high. She shook a finger at the man.

Constance stalked off, still visibly angry. The man moved on, too, almost running into Bill Lascelle. I thought perhaps Bill had approached the man, hoping to smooth over whatever had happened with Constance. But I was wrong. Neither looked at or gestured toward Constance. The men stood side by side, looking toward me as they talked, apparently amiably, for several minutes. Then, once again, the atmosphere turned frosty. Bill crossed his arms over his chest and talked in staccato bursts out of the side of his mouth. Jordan hovered in the background with a drink on a tray, uncertain whether to interrupt the men to deliver it. The man in the blazer shook his head vehemently, pointing into the crowd.

The two men moved apart abruptly. With a visible sigh of relief, Jordan gave the drink to Bill Lascelle.

I wondered if I had a problem on my hands. Was the man in the blazer a wedding crasher? Had he boarded the tour boat at the pier on a whim or with bad intent? We hadn't thought to have tickets or a checklist. It hadn't seemed necessary.

I worked my way into the tight circle around Zoey. "Is everything okay?" I inclined my head toward the man. He was once more moving through the crowd, chatting and laughing with one and all. The man saw me looking at him and started over, but the group closed around Zoey, and Amelia resolutely turned her back to him. I didn't think it was about him. It was about the group asserting their right to Zoey.

"Everything is wonderful." Zoey smiled her big, beautiful smile, genuinely happy. "Thank you so much."

I felt an arm come around my waist, and Tom's voice, calm and questioning, from behind. "Everything okay? It all seems great from out here."

"I'm slightly worried we may have a gate-crasher on our hands." I nodded toward the man in the blue blazer.

"Do you want me to take care of him?"

"No. Not yet. First I want to check with Jamie and Zoey to make sure he isn't invited."

"Okay. You let me know."

We walked together to ring the ship's bell that let people know it was time to find seats for the meal. There was some milling and more clumping, but soon everyone headed toward the picnic tables.

I glanced back up toward Windsholme. Mel, the tall caterer, and Cassie Howard were cleaning up tables and clearing away glasses. The man in the blue blazer was still up there, looking toward the picnic tables as if searching for a place to sit. Mel walked behind him, saying "Excuse me." That seemed to wake the man up, and he walked determinedly down the lawn, patting his hair in place.

CHAPTER FIVE

The guests sat with friends and family, as expected. Jamie's relatives and the locals favored the tables in the dining pavilion, open to the air but somewhat sheltered from the evening breezes. The artists sat at the tables on the lawn. It was less than three weeks from the longest day of the year, and the sky was still bright. Everyone would enjoy a beautiful sunset at the end of the meal.

The servers brought the first course, the New England clam chowder, and the guests dug in, many expressing their appreciation. The air had grown cooler, and there was a definite breeze. The warm, creamy, briny, flavorful soup was more than welcome.

I was slightly surprised that, when the man in the blue blazer finally sat down, it was at the table that held Jamie's parents and closest family. Dan, the groomsman, was on one side of him, Jamie's aunt and her husband on the other. Across from them were Jamie's parents and Dan's mom and dad, who, in the complicated geometry of the family, was also Jamie's oldest brother.

At least the question of who the stranger belonged to had been answered. He wouldn't have sat with the groom's parents if he wasn't connected to them. The man was chatting away with the family.

Jamie and Zoey did not sit down to eat but moved together from table to table, greeting guests they hadn't seen yet and chatting as well as the noise from many conversations allowed. I traveled from table to table too, answering questions about the Clambake and the wedding the next day, opening the bottles of champagne on each table as I went.

As the servers cleared away the clam-chowder bowls, the best man, Pete Howland, rose from his seat on the porch of the dining pavilion. He was five years older than Jamie, round-faced and snub-nosed. Short as a police officer could be, and chubby, he was the Jeff to Jamie's Mutt, the Hardy to Jamie's Laurel. Despite his stature, he managed to command everyone's attention.

"If you had told me, on Jamie's first day on the Busman's Harbor police, I'd be standing up as the best man at his wedding, I, well, I would have been skeptical. He was a skinny kid, greener than green, who had a college degree in criminal justice—always a useless commodity—and the strangest notions about how to drive a patrol car I'd ever seen." Pete pantomimed Jamie at the wheel, waving to pedestrians and cars to go ahead of him. "After you, sir. No, no, after you. After you." Pete paused for a beat, a master of comedic timing. "If you can't use a police car to barrel through traffic, I ask you, what is it good for?"

Most of the guests obligingly tittered at this.

"But over the last eight years, Jamie has become my partner and my best friend. He's saved my life twice, and there's no one I would rather have my back."

He turned toward Zoey, who stood next to Jamie looking a tiny bit apprehensive and puzzled, as though the best man's speech wasn't written down in her meticulous script for how the evening would go. Someone at the table next to where the happy couple stood had handed each a glass of champagne.

"When I met Zoey, I was similarly skeptical. What is it with Jamie and these small, ahty girls 'from away' he's so attracted to?" Pete pronounced it with an exaggerated Maine accent, and people did laugh. "But then I got to know her. She is one of the kindest, dearest, most genuine people I've ever met. And she loves my partner."

Pete raised his glass. "And so, Zoey, I relinquish my partner to be your partner. To have and to hold. Forever."

"Here, here." The guests raised their glasses and drank.

Jamie raised his glass to Pete, mouthing, "Thank you." They were both a little wet around the eyeballs.

Zoey raised her glass to her lips, faked taking a drink, and then set it on the table. Still pacing herself, I saw.

I stepped forward to tell the first tables to go to the clambake fire to pick up their meals, but didn't get that far because Dan's father rose. As he started in on reminiscences of Jamie as a pain-in-the-neck little brother, Sonny glared at me from the clambake fire and opened his mouth. I didn't need to hear what he was saying to know what it was. "If this is your idea of moving these people in and out of here quickly before the storm, you are doing a terrible job." I nodded and glared back. I was more than aware.

Mr. Dawes's speech ended to a smattering of applause and another toast. Again, Zoey picked up the glass, faked a sip, and set it down.

Out of the corner of my eye, I caught Constance Marshall, at a table full of artists, poised to stand. I ran over quickly and practically tackled her. To cover up, I sent her table to the clambake fire to pick up their meals and then continued calling the artists' tables on the lawn. I'd intended to send the group with Jamie's parents first, but the best-laid plans, et cetera, et cetera.

I sped past my family's table, where Tom sat with Mom, Captain George, the Snuggs, and Gus and Mrs. Gus. Tom caught my arm. "Can I help?"

I shook my head. "No, but thanks."

I saw Zoey headed to the restroom. Figuring my maid-of-honor job now took precedence, I grabbed one of our most experienced servers and asked her to continue calling the tables, and then followed Zoey into the bathroom.

"You're pregnant!" I stage-whispered as I entered the ladies' room. I hoped my tone indicated celebration, not accusation. As I'd jogged toward the restroom, all sorts of observations had swirled together in my head. The fact that Zoey was avoiding certain glazes in the studio. The rush to move up the date of the wedding. When was the last time I'd seen her drink anything alcoholic? She'd even rejected the Snuggs' deadly punch at her shower.

"Sssshhhh!" A hissing shush came from under the door of the middle stall. Then a louder and more cautious, "Is anybody else in here?"

I checked under the two other doors, something I should have done at the start. "Nope," I reported.

By then, Zoey was out of the stall and headed to the sink to wash her hands. Her eyes were bright, and her mouth was turned up in a smile. "Yes," she said, applying soap and rubbing her hands together. "Yes." She rinsed her hands and then she was in my arms.

"Are you happy?" I hardly needed to ask.

"So happy." She squeezed me tighter. "I love you."

"I love you, too." I let her go, and we both wiped away nearly shed tears.

"No one can know," she cautioned.

I felt my eyebrow go up, questioning. She couldn't be worried about people judging her. Her own mother had been unmarried. And she and Jamie were adults well into their thirties and fully committed to one another. Not like the last wedding when I'd been the maid of honor. Livvie, just out of high school, had married Sonny in front of the fireplace at my parents' house, Livvie looking like she'd swallowed a watermelon. They were two terrified, but defiant, teenagers. They weren't getting married to please either set of parents. In fact, my mom and dad and Sonny's widowed father had argued against it. But Livvie and Sonny's stubborn insistence had won the day. They wanted to be wed, and before the baby was born. They were legally old enough. There was nothing to do but give in. No one in the room would have ever guessed that they'd still be together today.

I was wondering idly if I was destined only to be maid of honor to expectant brides when Zoey answered the question I hadn't asked.

"Because this weekend is about the wedding," she said. "We planned and dreamed of it for so long. There'll be plenty of time to celebrate the baby later."

"Of course," I agreed. "When?"

The smile lit up her face again. "Early November. I can't wait." The smile disappeared as quickly as it had come. "I never had a family," she said. Something I knew well. "My mom was completely alone, and then she was gone. Now I have all this, this huge family." She waved her hand toward the lawn and dining pavilion, full of chattering people: Jamie's big family, Zoey's found family of artists. The local friends, yet another sort of family. She cupped her belly with her hand. "Since Mom died, I haven't known a single biological relation," she said, her voice low. "Soon I'll know one. It makes me so happy."

I hugged her once more, and we turned together, pushed the door of the ladies' room open, and walked back toward the cacophony of happy voices.

"Head up, shoulders back, smile," I told her. But I didn't need to. She was already standing straight and proud.

CHAPTER SIX

I left Zoey at a table with Jamie. Someone had
thoughtfully grabbed her a meal. She was the
bride, after all.

Everyone had their food and was back in their
places on the picnic benches. The conversation
had quieted as people focused on their lobsters. I
worked my way through the crowd, showing someone how to use the nutcracker on their lobster's
claws, tying on another person's bib, answering
questions about the meal and the history of the island. Servers ran to and fro with more water and
iced tea, and there was regular, but not overwhelming business at the bar.

All seemed to be going well when I heard a loud
thump and saw several of the people at Jamie's
parents' table jump up. The man in the blue
blazer had fallen backward off his bench.

"He's allergic!" a woman screamed. I didn't see
who.

The man lay on the deck of the dining pavilion,
gasping for air. I ran toward him, cursing under
my breath. He was bright red, clutching his throat.

My heart raced, fearing what could be happening. A massive allergic reaction to shellfish. I was always afraid of it on some level.

Tom beat me to the man, Jamie and Pete right behind him. Thanking every entity I could think of for the presence of trained professionals, I ran to the kitchen for the first-aid kit, in which we kept injectable epinephrin for just this sort of emergency. I yelled to Tom, Jamie, and Pete about where I was going as I went.

Tom was looking around, assessing the crowded room. People stood and stared, many hand to mouth. There was a chorus of concerned voices and offers of help. "We'll take him behind the counter of the gift shop," Tom called to me.

The gift shop, in the far corner of the dining pavilion, wasn't enclosed, but the high counter shielded its small floor space from view, and there were no tables nearby. Several people asked me what was happening as I rushed past with the first-aid kit. I assured them everything was fine as credibly as someone running with a first-aid kit could.

When I reached the gift shop, Pete was doing chest compressions, while Jamie timed him. I pulled the EpiPen from the packaging and handed it to Tom. "Are you sure?" I asked.

"No, but it's better to try it than just let him die here." Tom jabbed the needle into the man's thigh, right through his trousers.

The epinephrin appeared to have no result. My heart was beating so hard and fast, I was afraid I might keel over. Nothing like this had ever happened at the Clambake. And on Jamie and Zoey's special day.

Eventually, Jamie sat back on his heels, reaching

over to touch Pete's arm, halting the next compression. "He's gone," Jamie said.

"Oh, no!" It flew out of my mouth without passing through my brain. I'd known the man was dead, but some visceral part of me denied it.

Tom nodded in agreement. "Yeah." He looked at his watch. "8:05 p.m. The coroner will want to know."

"What do we do?" I asked.

Tom looked out from the open porch toward the sky. "We have dessert and get these people out of here before the storm comes. I'll call the Coast Guard and ask them to come pick up the body. Discreetly, as soon as the *Jacquie II* is gone."

Body retrieval wasn't the Coast Guard's responsibility, but they would come. They were helpful like that.

While all this had been taking place in our little corner, the conversation level in the dining pavilion had almost returned to the pre-dinner roar. People were finishing their meals. I peeked up over the counter. "Do we leave him here until then?" I asked.

Many of the guests were grabbing their drinks and heading to the west side of the island to watch the sunset. Cradled by a bank of fast-moving clouds, the sun shot rays of bright pinks and oranges far above the horizon. People oohed and aahed.

Tom poked his head over the gift-shop counter and looked around. "We'll carry him up to Windsholme. I'll stay with him there to keep out prying eyes. Pete and Jamie, I need your help to carry him, but then get back to the wedding as soon as you can. You'll be missed."

We reluctantly agreed to the plan. "Put him in the old billiards room." I turned to Jamie. "Who is he?"

Jamie looked at me blankly. "Why are you asking me?"

"Because it's your wedding and he was sitting at your parents' table," I answered, as puzzled by his reaction as he was by mine.

Jamie stared at the man again, whose face was at rest now that he'd stopped gasping for air. "I never saw him before tonight."

I was relieved to see, when I exited the gift-shop area, that the main course had been cleared and dessert was on all the tables. The staff, more in tune with Maine weather than guests from out of town, wanted to get on the boat and go home as much as I wanted this shindig to be over. In addition to the clouds, the wind had come up. It wasn't howling, or even steady, but strong enough that the guests at the unprotected tables on the lawn had shrugged into sweaters, jackets, or shawls. Down at the dock, I could hear the waves hitting the *Jacquie II*, and there was a smell of roiling saltwater that hadn't been there before.

Captain George rose as soon as he saw me. "We've got to get these people out of here."

I nodded my agreement, stepped onto the porch of the dining pavilion, and shouted until I had everyone's attention. "Thank you so much for coming to Zoey's and Jamie's rehearsal dinner at the Snowden Family Clambake Company. We hope you had a great time and enjoyed your meal." I paused for a moment to acknowledge the clapping and cheering that followed. I'd pandered for it, but still it was nice to hear. "We'll see you all tomorrow at 1:30 sharp at the town pier. Don't be late. Time and tide waits, and so on."

Jamie, just returned from moving the body, stepped up and thanked the cooks and the rest of the staff, the Snowden family, and so on for their efforts. He knew exactly what he was doing. He gave everyone time to finish dessert and then announced it was time to get on the boat.

As the crowd waited on the dock to walk single file across the gangway, everyone on the staff ran around like crazy, cleaning the rest of the paper bowls the blueberry grunt was served in, throwing utensils in plastic bins to soak, and stowing champagne and other glasses behind the bar. Sonny and his crew collected the remains of the meal and the rest of the garbage. It would go back to the mainland, hidden away on the *Jacquie II*. My niece, Page, jumped in to help. She'd be on the paid Clambake staff for the first time this summer.

I looked for the members of the wedding party who'd be staying overnight at Windsholme. I found Dan Dawes on the dock, saying good-bye to his parents and grandparents. He kissed the women and embraced the men. "See you tomorrow," he said, "the happy day."

I put a hand on his arm. "If you wait until I'm done here, I'll show you to your room. Your bag and wedding suit are already up there."

He nodded his agreement and thanks. I saw the rest of the guests onto the boat. Mom waved from the pilot house, where she stood next to Captain George. He blew the ship's horn and immediately pulled the *Jacquie II* away from the dock. I sighed with relief as the boat turned and headed toward Busman's Harbor.

CHAPTER SEVEN

D an Dawes was waiting by the steps that led up to the dining pavilion. "That was great tonight." He gave me a broad smile.

"I'm so glad you had fun."

"I'm sorry I missed the rehearsal. I was enjoying myself with my parents and grandparents and lost track of the time."

"You didn't miss much," I assured him. "Just stand at the front and look happy." He sounded sincerely sorry, but was he? Would a man like Dan, who'd grown and run a hugely successful company, lose track of the time?

We walked along in silence, crossing the great lawn toward Windsholme. The *Jacquie II* had left at quarter to nine. It was a bit of a bum's rush for the guests, many of whom would have liked to have stayed to party longer, but they'd all taken the move to the boat with good grace.

"That man who was next to you at dinner—" I started.

"The one who had the attack?" Dan's smile disappeared. "Is he all right?"

"No. He's not." There was no point in lying about it. I'd fended off several inquiries from guests as they boarded the boat. In those cases, I'd obfuscated. There would be more questions tomorrow, and we had to be prepared to respond to them. Truthfully. For the members of the wedding party, staying overnight, the truth telling started now.

"I haven't seen any sign of a rescue squad." Dan clearly understood what that meant.

So did I. "The Coast Guard is on the way to pick up the body."

He stopped walking and turned to me. "That must have been quite a shock for you."

"And for you, too." I was touched that his concern was for me. "You sat next to him at dinner."

We began to walk again. "It is a shock," Dan said. "It's hard to believe I was talking to the guy a couple of hours ago, and, boom, he's gone."

"Do you know who he is or who we should notify?"

Dan shook his head. "No idea. Nobody at our table knew him. He was the last one to sit down. There was one spot left." Dan smiled, but more tentatively this time. "Because I'm single and plus-one-less. I figured he had no one to sit with, so he grabbed the seat."

"Did he tell you his name?"

"He told us his name was Kendall Clarkson," Dan's smile turned apologetic. "I'm pretty sure. It was loud."

"Where was he from?"

"That I do know," Dan answered quickly. "LA—

we have that in common. That's what we chatted about, him and me, and my dad. The Dodgers and the Lakers."

"Do you know why the man was here? Was he a friend of Zoey's?" Given that Jamie and Dan didn't know him, and given the California connection, that was the most likely explanation.

"No idea."

Constance Marshall had talked to the dead man before sitting down to dinner. As had Bill Lascelle. They might know more. And I could ask Zoey, though I dreaded telling her the man was dead, if that unhappy task fell to me.

Dan and I walked the rest of the way to Windsholme in silence, each thinking our own thoughts. Mine were about the dead man and how fleeting life could be. I guessed Dan's ran along similar lines. The sun had gone down completely, and the rolling clouds had made quick work of the twilight. It was fully dark, but welcoming lights shone from the mansion's many windows, beckoning us inside.

I showed Dan to his room, one of three connected rooms that ran across the front of the second floor, appropriately known in its day as "the bachelors' quarters." In the late 1800s, when Windsholme was built, the unmarried men in the family and single, male guests were given those rooms. Jamie and Pete were also staying in that part of the house, and I was sure there would be some drinking and sentimental reminiscing this evening.

When I came back down the stairs, Jordan was in the big foyer, swinging his gym bag by the handles in front of his knees like a metronome. "Ms. Snowden!" He seemed happy to see me. "Livvie said you would tell me where my room is."

"Of course. Call me Julia." I was slightly embarrassed I hadn't got around to it before now. Jordan's presence meant that, back at the dining pavilion, cleanup was complete and everything stowed for the next day. Livvie would cook breakfast for our guests in the morning. She and her family were staying overnight in the little yellow house by the dock, where they lived in the summer.

I led Jordan to the third floor. It felt ironic to give him a room in the old servant's quarters, but it also made the most sense. There was only one finished washroom on this floor, but he wouldn't be sharing it with anyone.

"Is that man all right?" he asked. "The one who had the attack?"

I hadn't intended to bring the man up if Jordan didn't, but I'd told Dan and would be telling others soon. Jordan would hear it soon enough. "I'm sorry to tell you he's not. He died."

Jordan halted halfway up the stairs and stared at me. "He's dead? You're sure?"

I put a hand on his arm, though I barely knew him. He was really upset. "You waited on him, didn't you?"

Jordan gulped and wet his lips, as if trying to move some saliva back into a dry mouth. "I did. I brought him a drink from the bar just before it happened."

"Did he tell you his name? Or anything about himself?" Dan had said he thought the man's name was Kendall Clarkson. It would be nice to confirm it.

Jordan shook his head. "No. There wasn't time. It was really busy."

I smiled at that, trying to put him more at ease. "Yes, it was. Did you notice, did he eat his clam chowder?" The man's table had barely sat down from getting their lobsters when he'd fallen over. I doubted very much if he'd touched the lobster or the steamers. The swiftness of the attack puzzled me. Either he was allergic to all shellfish, and it was a slow reaction to the clams in the chowder, or it was an immediate reaction to the lobsters and clams on his plate. That was possible. Some people were so allergic they couldn't even touch shellfish. But if he had an allergy that severe, how could he not know about it?

"He ate the chowder." Jordan didn't have any trouble remembering. "It was when I cleared his bowl away that he asked me to go to the bar for him. He didn't eat his lobster. He didn't have time."

When we reached Jordan's room, I turned on the lights and showed him the way to the bathroom. I didn't want to leave him, but he'd calmed down considerably, and I had a lot of things to do.

Still puzzled about what had happened with the man, and the chowder, and the lobsters, I said goodnight to Jordan and made my way down one flight of stairs.

On the second floor, I followed the long hallway to my apartment, a feeling of dread pressing down on my stomach. It was past time to check in on Zoey. I was her maid of honor and should be with her.

I found her on the couch in my apartment, her ex-boyfriend Derek holding her hand. His plus-one, Amelia, sat on the window seat across from them, not even trying to hide her irritation.

I stopped in the doorway as soon as I saw them. I hadn't realized those two were still on the island. Normally, we would have counted the guests as they boarded the *Jacquie II* to make sure everyone was present. In the rush to get the guests off the island, evidently that hadn't happened. "Hello?"

All three of them looked at me as if I was the last person they expected to see in my own apartment. It was Derek who spoke. "We stayed to be with Zoey. She's had a stressful evening."

Was it my guilty conscience about my maid-of-honor duties that read criticism in his tone, or was it really there?

"You'll have to stay the night," I said. "The sea is much too rough for anyone to run you back." As if to punctuate my remark, there was a tap-tap of rain against the windows, followed at once by a wind-driven deluge.

"But my dress for the wedding," Amelia protested.

"My brother-in-law can run you back to town in the morning when he goes to pick up our employees. You can get changed and take the tour boat back here with the rest of the guests. For tonight, we'll find you a room."

I started mentally sorting out room assignments. There was another unexpected guest, Tom, who was, at that moment, presumably standing watch over the corpse. Tom had been scheduled to go home tonight. He'd said it was because I'd be spending my time with Zoey, which was true. But he was also reluctant to stay overnight on the island at any time, even when he was off duty. In conditions better than tonight's, you could travel from Morrow Island to Busman's Harbor in fifteen minutes if you knew the most direct route. But then, as Tom pointed out, when you got to town, you were at the end of one of Maine's long peninsulas, more than an hour from his office. And hours, potentially, from wherever he needed to be.

"What happened to that man, the one who had the attack?" Zoey's trembling voice brought me back to the moment.

No one had told her yet. I squared my shoulders, mentally giving Jamie a good talking to. Surely this was his job. I wasn't crazy about the fact that Derek and Amelia were in the room, but I couldn't figure out how to ask them to leave, especially since they couldn't retire to their room until I gave them one. "I'm sorry, but he's dead." I moved to stand by Zoey's side, the side away from Derek.

"*What!*" Amelia shouted.

I didn't repeat it. They had all heard me.

Zoey froze for a moment, as the information penetrated, and then burst into sudden, noisy sobs. Who wouldn't in her situation? She'd been planning for this day for months. She'd been dreaming of it even longer. All her life, it seemed to me. And now, awash in the hormones of early pregnancy, she faced a death at her rehearsal dinner. All brides wanted everything to be perfect. I patted her shoulder. She wiped her face with a tissue Derek handed her. "Where is he now?"

"In the billiards room. The Coast Guard is on

the way to pick him up." I wanted to reassure her that the corpse wouldn't be there in the morning.

"Do you think the wedding is ruined?" Zoey asked. "Does everyone know?"

"Of course not." Derek was vehement, and at the moment, he wasn't wrong.

But I couldn't imagine that the man's fate hadn't been a subject of speculation for many guests on the boat ride home. People would ask direct questions when they arrived the next day. Since the man wasn't a member of Jamie's family and seemed unconnected to Zoey's other friends, I held out the faint hope that his death wouldn't cast too much of a pall over the wedding day. Which reminded me . . . "Zoey, what is the man's name? Is there someone we should notify?"

Zoey blinked away her tears and shook her head. "I don't know him at all."

CHAPTER EIGHT

I showed Derek and Amelia to a room on the third floor. Amelia took one look, tossed her head, and sighed. The room was small, a former servant's quarters, and the bathroom was down the hall; they'd be sharing with Jordan. The furniture was sparse, a double bed on an old metal frame, a single nightstand and two hard wooden chairs. At least there was furniture, which wasn't the case with all the rooms on this floor.

I had a transitory guilty flash. I'd saved a better room on the second floor for Tom. But he'd been forced here by circumstances. He wasn't an uninvited guest.

Mom's employee discount at Linens and Pantries, where she worked in the off-season, ensured that we had plenty of sheets. I'd grabbed some before we climbed up from the second floor. I'd also grabbed a couple of clean Snowden Family Clambake Company T-shirts, which I kept around in case of emergencies. I thought this qualified.

I deposited the sheets and a wool blanket on the

bed and gave them the T-shirts. The rain was deafening under the roof. Amelia and Derek hung back with every expectation that I'd make up the bed. Instead, I moved away from it. "I hope you have everything you need. Breakfast will be eight o'clock until nine in the dining room. Coffee will be up at six and available all morning." I pointed out the door to the bathroom down the hall.

"We don't have toothbrushes," Amelia blurted.

I didn't know what she thought I could do about that. They were the ones who had missed the boat. I gave them my best smile, said, "I'm so sorry," and escaped into the hallway and down the stairs.

I found Tom, Jamie, and Pete in the old men's billiards room with the corpse. The room had originally been where gentlemen went for cigars and cards or other amusements after dinner, where they wouldn't be disturbed by the fairer, yet somehow weaker sex. In the renovation, we had turned it into a large dressing room for brides and their attendants. Zoey wouldn't be using it. She, Livvie, and I would dress in my apartment.

"Everyone is settled, I—" I entered the room talking, but stopped abruptly when I saw the three men. Each was staring at the corpse in a contemplative manner. Tom had his arms folded, one hand under his chin. Jamie had his hands in his pockets, neck jutting forward. And Pete held an open palm to his forehead.

Tom looked at me. "Does that look like an allergic reaction to you?"

"I'm not a doctor," I answered reflexively, but nevertheless stepped forward to look.

The man lay on his back, as though asleep, but blue around the lips and fingertips. There was nothing of the telltale swelling, redness, or rash I would have expected from a massive allergic reaction. "No," I admitted, "it doesn't, at least not to me."

"Not to any of us, either." Jamie pulled his hands out of his pockets and let his arms swing at his sides. "There's no medic-alert bracelet. He isn't carrying an EpiPen, at least that we've found so far. Why did we think it was a reaction?"

"Because a woman yelled, 'He's allergic,' and he was gasping for air," I answered. "His waiter told me the man had eaten his clam chowder but hadn't touched his lobster."

"So not an instantaneous reaction to the clams," Jamie said.

"No. The chowder had been eaten and the dishes cleared at least fifteen minutes before he got his meal. His table was the last one to be called."

Everyone nodded, faces still thoughtful.

"Do we know who the woman was?" I asked. "The one who screamed it was an allergy."

Jamie and Pete shook their heads.

"More to the point, did the woman know who *he* is?" Tom asked. "Or know anything about him, like that he might have a shellfish allergy."

"She couldn't have known him well," I pointed out. "If you were a friend, you wouldn't go back on the boat without at least inquiring how he was doing."

"He was on his own all evening," Jamie said. "I noticed that."

"Me, too. He was friendly, chatted with lots of people, but wasn't attached to any group." I looked at Tom. "What now?" He would know if any of us did.

"He's going to the medical examiner's office in Augusta for sure," Tom said. "Even without our doubts about an allergic reaction, he was probably headed there anyway. Sudden death, unknown identity, even though there were plenty of witnesses. I'll call ahead to let them know."

As his thumbs hovered over the screen, the phone rang, bursting into the tension in the room so discordantly that I jumped, heart thumping.

Tom put the phone to his ear, said, "Uh-huh," three times and then, "I understand. Good luck to you. Be safe."

"What now?" My stomach tensed again.

Tom lowered his hand with the phone still in it. "That was the Coast Guard. They won't be coming to pick up our corpse tonight. With this storm, they have their hands full taking care of living people and living people's property. They apologized and said they'd try to get here before the wedding guests tomorrow."

"The marine patrol or even the harbormaster can handle it in the morning," Jamie said.

Tom rolled his shoulders. Whatever happened, we were stuck with the corpse overnight.

The man's blazer was slung over the chair that went to the vanity table we'd put in place for the season's brides. Pete and Jamie had taken it off during the first-aid efforts and not put it back on. Tom picked the jacket up and felt all the pockets. "No wallet here," he announced. He went to the corpse and gently inserted his fingers into each of the front pants pockets, then stepped back, shaking his head.

"I walked back to the house with Dan Dawes earlier," I told them. "He happened to be sitting next to, er, him"—I pointed to the dead man—"when he fell over. Dan thinks the man's name is Kendall Clarkson, but he couldn't be sure."

Jamie raised his eyebrows at me. We'd each seen the invitation list about a hundred times. He didn't remember that name, either.

"Dan felt sure the man was from LA," I finished.

"One of Zoey's friends," Pete suggested.

"Zoey doesn't know him either." This drew a sharp look from Tom.

Before I'd arrived, the guys had turned on a few table lamps that barely lit the big room. I felt like a participant in some eerie, pagan ceremony as the four of us stood in our semicircle, looking at the body.

As if he'd read my mind, Tom said, "Julia, would you put the overhead light on?"

I did as he asked, turning on the fancy chandelier and pushing the dimmer switch to the max.

Without being asked, Jamie and Pete stepped forward and rolled the corpse onto one side so Tom could check the back pockets.

"Ah-ha!" Tom pulled a brown wallet out of the man's pocket and waved it in the air. The wallet was thin and worn at the edges. Tom opened it and rifled through the contents. "Kendall Clarkson," he read. "Address in Los Angeles."

I went over to look. The license photo was indeed the dead man. He was a little younger, had less white in his hair, and didn't have a mustache, but he was unmistakable.

"Five-ten, a hundred and fifty pounds, hair white, eyes brown. That's him," Tom said.

Jamie and Pete were slowly and carefully rolling Kendall Clarkson onto his back "Whoa! Stop." Jamie's tone demanded obedience, and Pete froze, his hands on the man's hips. "Look at this." Jamie was clearly addressing Tom, but I went over to look, too.

"Is that a needle mark?" Jamie pointed.

My eyes followed Jamie's finger. When the body had been rolled over, the man's thick, white hair had fallen back, exposing a tiny dimple behind his ear. We all peered at it, even Pete, who had to crane his neck to do so without letting go of the hips. The dimple was red and recent, with a small hole at its center.

"Yup," Tom agreed, "that's what that is."

There was a moment of stunned silence. As if to punctuate it, the wind roared, pushing a torrent of rain against the windows. "What does that mean?" My mouth was so dry, I could barely get the words out.

Tom already had his phone in hand. "It's not a place where you'd inject yourself. There are undoubtedly a lot of possible explanations. But I've seen a case like this before. This man was probably murdered." He took his phone from his pocket again and pressed the screen. The three of us stared at him. I couldn't think of anything else to do.

Tom put the phone to his ear, shook his head, and then lowered the phone, squinting at it. "No service," he said. "No cell, no internet." The wind howled again as if to highlight his words. "We're on our own."

CHAPTER NINE

I exhaled noisily, as if pushing out air would push out the dread that felt like a hard, cold stone in my stomach. Unfortunately, I had more than a passing knowledge of murder investigations. One thing seemed highly doubtful: that we would be having a wedding the next day.

"We shouldn't have moved him," Pete said.

"We thought it was an allergic reaction." Tom was unapologetic. "Besides," he looked at the dark windows, the wind-driven rain thrumming against them, "the medical examiner will be glad we got him out of the storm." He looked at Jamie and Pete. "I'll defend it if I have to."

"We have to tell Zoey," Jamie said. "She needs to know."

"What?" I was startled into the present moment, my mind ticking. "Don't we need to tell everyone here that he was murdered?" I waved my hands in the air, gesturing toward all the rooms, nooks, and crannies in Windsholme. "We may be locked in this house with a killer."

"Or," Jamie's expression was grim, "we just sent a murderer back to Busman's Harbor with everyone in the world we care about and no way to warn anybody."

The hairs on the back of my neck stood up, and my arms broke out in gooseflesh. I was about to protest, but then looked at Tom. He would know what to do.

Tom's dark brows wrinkled together over his nose, a sure sign he was thinking things through, weighing pros and cons, and figuring out what should happen from here on. "We have two choices," he said. "I can sit here guarding the corpse all night, and we can wait until the Major Crimes Unit gets here in the morning." He paused while we absorbed this. "Or, since we have a Major Crimes detective here and two very capable local officers," he looked at me, "and one very capable amateur, we can try to get a jump on understanding what happened while people's memories are fresh." His tone left little question as to which route he preferred.

"How do we do that?" I asked.

Tom looked toward the windows that lined the outside wall. The wind obligingly howled, pushing rain against the glass, reminding us of what was going on outside. "We won't be able to search the scene," Tom said, unnecessarily. "If there's anything left of it. What time is it?"

I pulled out my otherwise useless phone. "A few minutes after ten."

"Most folks will still be up," Tom said, weighing his words. "Especially those on West Coast time. Let's find out as much about the victim as we can. We don't want to give people more information than we have to. We're the only ones who know it was murder, aside from the killer. It's one of our few advantages in this situation. We'll tell people we're trying to figure out the man's identity."

"We know his identity," I protested.

"No one knows we know that," Tom answered.

"But won't we be endangering people," I asked, "if we don't tell them that they're in the house with a murderer?"

"*May* be in the house with a murderer," Tom responded. "We aren't sure this was murder, and we don't know if the person who did it is still here. We're only looking for information. Besides, this would appear to be a targeted attack. Whatever killed him had to be brought onto the island, along with the syringe. I doubt very much the perpetrator is a danger to others unless he or she feels threatened or surprised."

"Great," I restrained myself from rolling my eyes.

"We'll tell everyone to lock their doors," Tom said.

We all smiled at that, even Jamie. "That won't make them suspicious at all," he said. "What about Zoey?"

"We won't tell her we suspect murder." Tom's tone was tight and professional. He knew what he was asking of Jamie.

"Unacceptable," Jamie said immediately.

Tom didn't respond right away, his detective self warring with his friend self. I was enormously relieved when he gave in.

"Okay," Tom said. "Jamie and Julia, you talk to Zoey. Jamie's right. She should know, and you're the ones who should tell her. Pete and I will stay

here to guard the body." He looked at Jamie and
me, face serious. "Stay together." It was a command. "I don't want any of us wandering around
alone."

I didn't like it. I didn't want to do any of it. I
dreaded telling Zoey, whose carefully planned,
deeply desired picture-book wedding was already
under threat from the storm and Mr. Clarkson's
death. A murder would make the island a crime
scene, one containing witnesses and suspects. I
couldn't see how we'd be having a wedding tomorrow.

Jamie and I climbed the stairs and walked down
the long second-floor hall toward my apartment.
Neither of us talked, and I could tell his mind was
churning, as mine was, headed to the same in-
evitable conclusion. The hallway had rooms on either side, and with the third floor above, I could
barely hear the storm. The loudest sound was the
creak of our footsteps on the old oak floor.

The power was still on, thank goodness. Our
electricity came over in a conduit that ran under
the sea from Westclaw Point. As long as the mainland had power—by no means a sure thing, considering the nearest piece of the mainland was at
the end of a peninsula—we would have power. In
the renovation, we'd installed a generator, which
would keep the big restaurant refrigerator and
freezer and a few select lights going if we did lose
power. That would keep the food for the wedding
feast fresh—in the unlikely event that there was
still a wedding tomorrow.

We'd reached my apartment door. Jamie tapped lightly. Zoey called softly, "Come in."

She'd moved from the couch to the window seat, where she sat in her pink rehearsal dress with a gray comforter Vee Snugg had knitted for me across her knees. There was an open box of tissues next to her and dozens of used ones wadded up and strewn over the window seat and floor.

Constance Marshall was in the room. She rose from the couch as Jamie and I entered. She'd changed into a pale blue terry bathrobe, zippered down the front, and had unfastened her long gray hair. It swung as she moved. She walked over to Zoey and squeezed her forearm. "I'm going to my room. Call if you need me."

I opened my mouth to say there was no cell service and therefore we couldn't call, but decided against it. I'd put Constance in the room next to my apartment. It would be a simple matter to walk down the hall and knock on the door if Jamie and I thought Zoey shouldn't be alone when we had to leave her.

Jamie went to Zoey and gathered her into his arms on the window seat. I grabbed a kitchen chair and pulled it next to them.

"What?" Our serious faces were scaring her, but she had to be told.

"Honey," Jamie started, "the man at dinner, the one who we thought died of an allergic reaction . . . now we think he may have been murdered."

"Murdered!" Zoey shouted, radically altering the mood in the room.

I couldn't blame her. I would've shouted too, if I hadn't found out when I was surrounded by cops. I glanced over my shoulder at the door to the hallway, which Constance had closed behind her. I didn't think anyone could have heard Zoey unless they happened to be lingering directly outside the apartment door.

Jamie reached for the box and handed Zoey another tissue. She wasn't crying at the moment, but he must have anticipated it would be needed.

Zoey, however, didn't collapse. "How?" she asked. Her voice still wavered, but she was very much in control.

"We don't know, exactly," Jamie answered. "But we suspect poison. Administered by injection."

Zoey made a mewling sound. I leaned forward in the chair and took her hand. "Did you know him?" I asked.

A tear formed on her lower eyelid and ran down next to her nose. "No. I told you before." She stared at me. Annoyed at the repetition of the question? Defensive?

"Honey," Jamie shifted on the seat and hugged her closer, "his name is Kendall Clarkson. He's from Los Angeles." He didn't ask a direct question, and Zoey didn't respond, so he continued. "I looked at that invitation list dozens of times and the seating chart just as many. I don't remember that name. Do you?"

Zoey shook her head, which caused a tear to fly off her nose. "No."

"It's just," Jamie tried one more time, "the Los Angeles connection. I thought he might be one of yours. Someone from home you invited at the last minute."

Zoey's wet eyes flashed angrily at Jamie. "You

have guests from LA, too. Your Uncle Dick and his whole family. Your groomsman nephew, Dan, for goodness' sake."

"I understand." Jamie stroked her hair. "But I don't know the dead man."

Zoey was definite. "Neither do I."

I stood up, not sure what else to do. Jamie looked up, then hugged Zoey tighter. "I'm going to walk Julia downstairs to Tom. Then I'm coming right back. Lock the door behind us."

Zoey looked momentarily puzzled. "We weren't going to be together the night before the wedding," she said to Jamie. "We agreed—" Her face rearranged itself two or three times as the truth dawned on her. There probably wasn't going to be a wedding tomorrow. The event she had longed for, planned for, counted on, wasn't going to happen. The obvious conclusion hit her like a frying pan to the face. After a moment of stunned, openmouthed silence, she burst into noisy sobs.

"I can go by myself," I said to Jamie. "You watch me to the end of the hallway from here. Then I'll call to Tom. He'll be able to hear me from the stairs." I wasn't certain that was true. The billiards room was three huge rooms away from the stairway, and both doors to it were closed. But I didn't want Zoey to be left alone.

Neither did Jamie. He let go of Zoey and came toward the doorway. "Go ahead," he whispered.

CHAPTER TEN

"Tom!" I called from the top of Windsholme's grand staircase, steadying myself on the newel post. "Tom!"

My words disappeared into a sweep of rain against the two-story window behind the lower landing and the large oval foyer below. We'd rehearsed the wedding there hours earlier, when the sun was out, and we were planning for a beautiful day. I looked back at Jamie, framed in the doorway of my apartment. He nodded encouragingly.

I put a foot on the first step, cautiously and slowly, but then decided going fast was the better approach. I flew down the stairs, through the foyer, then the dark main salon, where the round tables were already set for the wedding dinner, to the door of the billiards room. My hands were shaking at the idea of being on my own, and I couldn't turn the knob on the first try. *Julia, get ahold of yourself.* I got it on the next try, and the door swung open.

Pete was seated in one of the room's comfortable chairs, meant for brides, their mothers, or attendants. The chair was a satiny pink, and he looked ridiculous in it. Tom was standing and turned quickly as I entered the room. "Where's Dawes?"

"He stayed with Zoey." The look on Tom's face caused me to quickly add, "She isn't good."

Tom looked like he was going to speak, but then shut his mouth, nodding.

"Now what?" I asked.

"Pete will stay with Mr. Clarkson," Tom said. "You and I will start talking to witnesses."

I looked over at Pete, comfy in his chair. He was a notoriously early riser, who suffered through his occasional obligations to take the night shift. He was the best man, and though I'd noticed he'd stuck to beer, I wasn't sure how much he'd drunk. At least, whatever he'd had, he'd had it a couple of hours ago. A couple of sobering hours in every sense.

Pete noticed me looking at him and waved a hand. "I'll be fine."

Tom had already started for the door, but turned back when Pete spoke. "He'll be fine," Tom said. "I want you with me."

I would have liked to think it was because he wanted my keen insights into human nature during the interviews, but a more likely explanation was he didn't want me out of his sight. I didn't want him out of my sight either. He might've been a trained professional, but there was always safety in numbers. I followed him out the door.

"Who first?" I asked.

"Unless you think anyone in particular has information, we pick person number one randomly and keep going."

We were on the second floor by then, headed down the hallway. "The art teacher," I suggested. "Constance Marshall. She is, or probably was, the officiant. She's from California, where she taught Zoey in high school. I saw her talking to the dead man during the cocktail party. It got a little heated."

"Good enough," Tom said, as we stopped outside her door. He gave it a hard rap with his knuckles.

Constance opened the door right away, no doubt assuming it was Jamie, summoning her to stay with Zoey. "Oh." She stepped back into the room, surprised.

Tom entered with me right behind him. There were two chairs in the room in addition to the bed. One was at a small writing desk, the other a leather easy chair. There was a paperback book, upside down and open on the side table, and the reading lamp was on. Constance had clearly been sitting there, keeping herself awake with a book in case Zoey needed her.

The day's cast-off clothes were draped over the back of the desk chair. I knew Tom wouldn't want to have this conversation while standing, because it would signal we needed to be gone as quickly as possible. He'd want Constance to have the impression we would stay as long as it took.

I removed the clothes from the back of the wooden chair, placing them on the desk, and turned the chair to face the room. Tom understood what I was doing and sat in it immediately. I sat on the still-made bed, thinking, correctly as it turned out, that the natural thing for Constance to do would be to go back to the easy chair, where she was obviously comfortable.

When we were all seated, Tom leaned forward, elbows on his knees, hands steepled in front of him. "You saw the man who unfortunately was taken ill during dinner?" he asked Constance.

She nodded, serious. "I did. Zoey told me he died. I'm so sorry."

"Unfortunately, no one seems to be able to provide information about his identity." Tom's tone was as serious as hers. "Like who his next of kin might be. People who need to be notified, that sort of thing. We're trying to help with that."

Constance nodded. "And you are?" She looked at me on the bed. "I know Julia, but . . ."

A flash of lightning through the window behind her made me jump. "I'm sorry," I said. "I've misplaced my manners. This is—" Thunder rumbled in the background. Pretty far away. It was early in the year for thunderstorms, but not impossibly so. Obviously.

"I apologize," Tom put in before I could speak again. He paused long enough for me to wonder whether he would give his title. "I'm Tom Flynn. I'm with the Maine State Police. I'm here because I'm Julia's boyfriend. And a friend of Jamie and Zoey's."

He'd told her he was police, but not a detective. He'd also conveyed that he was here for the wedding and not on duty, which was certainly true.

I cleared my throat lightly. "At the cocktail party, I saw you speaking to the gentleman who died. And we wondered whether he had told you anything that might help us reach his family."

When I'd moved the clothes, I'd noticed Constance's phone plugged in on the desk. If she'd been reading her book, there was a chance, just a small one, that she didn't realize we'd lost internet and phone connection to the mainland and therefore couldn't reach the man's family at the moment.

"We did speak," Constance confirmed, "although briefly and superficially, I'm afraid."

"But he introduced himself," Tom prompted. Clearly Constance was a stickler for proper introductions.

"He told me his name was Kendall Clarkson," she said, "and he was from Los Angeles, like me."

"What did you talk about?" Tom asked.

"Well, about art," Constance said, as if there were no other topic. "I told him I taught art, and he said he owned a gallery in Los Angeles, not far from where I live. I described my art for him as best I could and showed him a couple of photos on my phone, though that hardly does them justice. He said he might be interested in showing my work, and I should come by with some paintings."

"Your paintings are?" I asked.

"Oils. Mostly California landscapes."

"Did he give you a business card," Tom asked, "so you could contact him?"

"He didn't have any with him. It was a social occasion. He did tell me the name of the gallery, Kendall's, so I could look it up."

"Thank you," Tom said. "That's very helpful." Though it wouldn't do us any good tonight. "You said the gallery wasn't far from you. Had you ever been there?" It did make sense that an art teacher would visit a gallery in her neighborhood.

"It isn't so close," Constance said. "When he mentioned the name, I had a vague feeling of driving by the place, but I'm sure I've never been."

"It seemed like you and Mr. Clarkson might have had a disagreement," I said. "What was it about?"

She didn't react badly to the question, intrusive as it was, but merely waved it away with a swipe of her hand. "It was nothing. He complained he hadn't had a chance to talk to Zoey yet this evening." Constance shook her head, and her long gray hair moved like a curtain in the breeze, peeking out from behind her on either side. "I told him it was Zoey's wedding. I was sure she'd get to everyone, but tonight she was with friends she hadn't seen in ages. I told him not to be so selfish."

I smiled despite the seriousness of the conversation. I remembered her shaking finger, scolding the man like the schoolteacher she was.

Tom rose. "Thank you. You've been very helpful. If you think of anything else, you can let me know in the morning."

I stood as well, and we headed for the door. Tom paused, swinging it open. "I'm police, so I tell everyone the same thing all the time. Lock your door."

I looked at Constance, who was also standing. She seemed amused and not alarmed. I didn't put the chances of her complying at more than fifty-fifty. "He does say that," I echoed. "All the time."

She smiled and nodded, closing the door behind us. We stood silently, listening for the lock, which finally clicked into place.

*   *   *

"Who now?" I asked Tom as we stood in the hall-way outside Constance Marshall's door.

"We keep going. The later it gets, the more likely people are to be sleeping. Who else have you got on this floor?"

I pointed to the room across the hall from Constance's. "Jamie," I said. "Then Pete. Next to Pete, Jamie's nephew Dan. Bill Lascelle is on the other side of the hall next to Constance. I put you at the end of that row. Do you want to see your—"

"Thank you." He pecked me on the forehead. "But I don't know if I'll be using a bedroom tonight. Let's try nephew Dan. Do you know him?" We were already walking toward Dan's door.

"I used to know him when we were kids and he came to Busman's Harbor to visit his grandparents, but until tonight, I'd hadn't seen him in"—I did some quick calculating—"twenty years. His name is Daniel Dawes. He lives in California, grew up there, though he's been to Busman's Harbor often to visit family. And he was sitting right next to Mr. Clarkson when his attack began."

"That guy. I saw him when I first reached the victim."

"Did you notice anything particular about him?"

"Yeah. He didn't look surprised or upset, and he didn't make a move to help."

"Hmm."

Tom knocked on Dan's door. No answer. Tom knocked again. Harder. "Where could he be?"

I put my ear to the door. "In the shower?" I didn't hear a thing, and even if I could have, there would be no way to distinguish the sound of the shower from the sound of the rain against the bedroom windows. I turned to Tom and shrugged. "Pete's room connects to his. I doubt it's locked. We could go in that way."

Tom gave a sharp shake of his head. "It hasn't come to that. We won't be sneaking into Mr. Dawes's room. He needs to admit us. The connecting doors can be locked, right?"

I nodded.

"Then let's hope Mr. Dawes locked his, like a sane person. Who's next?"

I crossed the hall to the room next to Constance Marshall. "Bill Lascelle. He's playing the guitar for the ceremony tomorrow. He's an old friend of Zoey's, a mentor."

"Where's he from?"

"Denver. I did see him talking to Mr. Clarkson during the cocktail party."

Tom nodded that he'd understood and then knocked.

Bill Lascelle opened the door right away. He was still dressed in casual pants and the collared, cotton shirt he'd worn at the rehearsal dinner. He'd added a navy-blue sweater.

"I'm Tom Flynn," Tom said, not making the same mistake twice. "You know Julia."

Bill looked at me, the questions clear on his face. "We met at the rehearsal, yes."

"I'm with the Maine State Police," Tom said. "Can we come in and speak to you for a moment?"

Lascelle's brows flew up to his hairline. Like his temples, the brows were laced with gray. He said, "Of course," and stepped backward, out of the doorway. We followed him in, and Tom shut the door.

There was a laptop open on the desk and a phone plugged in beside it. Bill closed the laptop before he sat on the bed, gesturing for Tom and me to take the chairs. "To what do I owe the honor?" He was relaxed, smiling, and deeply curious. He didn't seem like a man who had anything to hide.

"You were acquainted with the man who was taken ill at dinner." Tom said it as a statement, not a question.

"Acquainted is a strong word," Bill responded. "I talked to him briefly during the cocktail hour. Why do you ask?"

"I am sorry to tell you he's dead." Tom's tone was very formal, serious, cop-like.

Bill was clearly taken aback. I would have sworn he was surprised. "How terrible. Was it an allergic reaction? That was the rumor this evening."

"I'm not a doctor," Tom said, perfectly straight-faced. After all, it was true. "I prefer not to speculate." That was a total lie.

Bill shifted on the bed. "How can I help?"

"We're trying to find some background on the dead man."

Bill was immediately skeptical. "Why are you gathering background, as you say? We have no phone or internet. There's no way for you to communicate back to the mainland."

Tom was silent for a moment, clearly weighing what he should and shouldn't say. "We're gathering information so when the victim goes back to the mainland tomorrow, we can send it along with him to make the medical examiner's job easier."

"You mean he's still here?" Lascelle wasn't alarmed. He seemed like a cool, calm guy, which made his angry words with the victim earlier in the evening even more interesting.

"Until the morning," Tom said. "Because of the storm. Tell me, what did you speak about?"

"Everything and nothing," Bill said. "The weather in Maine. Where we're from. How great the bride and groom are. Wedding small talk."

"What did he say about the bride and groom?" I asked, especially since neither of them claimed to know him.

"The usual stuff. Handsome couple." Bill paused for a moment, considering. "He said he'd never met Jamie."

"But he did know Zoey?" I pressed.

Bill shrugged, which caused him to bounce a little on the mattress. "I assumed. He didn't say he didn't know her. He must have known someone to be invited, right?"

That appeared to be a good question.

"Did the man tell you his name?" Tom asked.

"Yes," Lascelle said, "but I'm not sure I recall it correctly. Kent Clark? No, that can't be it. I'm thinking of Superman."

I smiled at the joke. "Did he say what he did for a living?"

Lascelle cast his eyes heavenward, as if remembering was a chore. The conversation had happened only five hours earlier. "I think he said he had owned a gallery in LA in the past, but now he was retired. That gave us some common ground because I show pieces in galleries from time to time."

"I thought you ran a business like Zoey's," I said, surprised.

"That's true. I have a commercial pottery business in Denver. We do large volume in-house and license our designs to manufacturers that sell worldwide. Zoey worked for me a few years ago. We became friends, and she's called on me from time to time as she's built Lupine Design."

"For design advice or business advice?" I was taking us off track, but I was genuinely curious. Tom shifted with impatience in his seat.

"Both," Bill answered, "though not so much recently about the business." He looked at me. "I understand you're running that side of Lupine now."

I agreed that I was and told him that after the wedding, I'd like to connect with him. I'd love to have someone who was successful in the space to ask for advice. He looked pleased.

"If you're a commercial potter, what did you have to discuss with a gallery owner or a former gallery owner?" Tom put us back on track.

"I also do one-of-a-kind, fine-art pieces that are in many galleries and a few museums, I'm proud to say."

That was interesting, the combination of art and commerce, practicing on both sides of an artificial divide.

"You were seen having an argument with the deceased," Tom said. "What caused that?"

Bill didn't answer right away. Finally, he spoke. "He annoyed me. He said something about ceramics couldn't be fine art. It was an ignorant thing to say, especially for someone who claimed to have owned an art gallery. I set him straight."

I couldn't decide if Mr. Clarkson had a talent for getting under people's skin, or if Constance and Bill were particularly sensitive. It seemed like it might be both.

"Did you see or talk the man after the cocktail party?" Tom asked.

"No. I didn't see him again until he was flat on the ground, and you were dragging him behind that counter while the best man pounded on his chest." Lascelle crossed his arms. "Is there anything else I can help you with?"

Tom stood up. "No, thank you."

I followed suit. "Let me know if you need anything. Towels, water, another blanket."

"Internet would be good," Bill said. "I'm trying to do a bit of business back home. But I doubt there's anything you can do about that." He gestured toward the window, which framed a black sky and transmitted the drumbeat of the rain.

"No, I'm sorry."

At the door, Tom said his thing about locking it. Bill's eyebrows rose again, but his hand was on the knob on his side of the door. "Goodnight," he said and closed it. The click of the lock followed immediately.

CHAPTER ELEVEN

"Neither of those conversations were particularly helpful," I said once we'd moved away from Bill's door.

Tom stopped walking and looked at me. "Ah, but they were," he said. "Now we know that both of them are lying."

"How do you know that?"

Tom put a hand behind his head and applied pressure to his neck. He'd had a long day, too. "Maybe not lying, but not telling the whole truth. Constance was wound tight as a clock. Bill was unnaturally calm. Neither gave a satisfactory explanation for the sharp words you witnessed."

I wanted to follow up on that, but by then we'd crossed the hall and Tom was knocking on Dan Dawes's door again. There was still no answer. Tom put his ear to the door, then frowned, though whether with puzzlement or concern, I couldn't tell. He rattled the doorknob, with no results. "Where now?" he asked me.

"Third floor. Friends of Zoey's. Also from California. But I'm not sure why we'd talk to them. I never saw them with our Mr. Clarkson. They were glued to Zoey's side all evening. When I came upstairs the first time, they were in my apartment with her. He's an ex of Zoey's." That got me a cocked eyebrow. "Her college boyfriend. I have the impression he's not over her. Wait until you see his girlfriend."

"I noticed." Tom widened his eyes at me. He'd seen the same resemblance I had. Of course, he had. Noticing was his business and not something he could turn off.

When we reached the top of the stairs, I led him to their room and knocked.

"Just a minute!" Derek called from inside. "Who is it?"

I looked at Tom, who nodded for me to speak. "It's Julia. And my boyfriend, Tom. I just want to check on—"

I was saved from having to make up something to check on when the door swung open.

Amelia was in the bed, a sheet pulled around her. I was relieved to see she was wearing the Snowden Family Clambake T-shirt. Derek was bare-chested, wearing the shorts he'd worn to the rehearsal, which were askew and obviously hastily pulled on for the purposes of opening the door.

"Sorry to disturb," Tom said smoothly, with the air of a man who has been met at a door many times by half-naked people, which, undoubtedly, he had.

Tom introduced himself, again carefully without using the word *detective*, and explained we were gathering information about the man who had the medical incident at dinner.

"He died," Derek said. "Julia told us."

"Yes," Tom acknowledged, "that's true."

"Why are you talking to us?" Amelia was the more hostile of the two of them.

"Did either of you talk to him before it happened?" Tom asked. "Maybe on the boat or at the cocktail party?"

"No," Amelia called from the bed, in a tone meant to end conversation.

"No," Derek reiterated, his voice a little friendlier, or at least curious. "Why? Is he a friend of Zoey's?"

I wasn't sure how Tom would handle that, but Derek answered his own question. "Must be if he's from California."

"That's where you know Zoey from, right?" I butted in. "You met in college." I'd intended the remark to lead in to a conversation. Instead, it came out more like a non sequitur.

Derek didn't seem concerned with the niceties of conversational flow. "Yeah. Cal Arts. We met our first day of freshman year. Zoey was just so cool."

A loud sigh came from the bed. The kind of sigh you make when your grandpa winds up to tell you a story for the fifty-seventh time.

Derek was undeterred. "I didn't know her history then. About her mom and the foster homes and all. Later freshman year, she had to testify in court against her mother's killer. She was so tough, but she needed support. I needed to protect her."

He talked in terms of his need, not Zoey's. He needed to protect her, but did she need his protection? Still, it helped me understand Zoey's loyalty to this ex. She was tough, but confronting her mother's killer, a man she loathed and had lived in the same small apartment with, must have been unbelievably stressful. And to do it when she was in college miles away from where she'd grown up. She'd aged out of the foster system. She had no support. I could see her needing someone to lean on.

"You were an art student like Zoey," I said. "What do you do now?"

Amelia answered instead of Derek. "He's an artist's agent. A big-deal one."

Derek blushed modestly. "I had the eye and the hand of an artist, but not the personality. I couldn't stand to be alone in a studio all day long. I needed to be out, talking to people, making connections, you know? Sort of by accident, I learned to use my artist's eye in a different way. A lot of what I do now is putting artists together with manufacturers, doing deals that way. I've been telling Zoey for years she should have her stuff manufactured in China, go for volume, big retailers, Target, Home Goods, and the like. I've done that for other clients."

Zoey's pottery was hand-thrown by her or by an artist in her studio or made in a mold to her exacting specifications. Though the dinnerware came in sets, each piece was unique. That's what made it special. On the other hand, mass manufacturing would make her designs available to a lot more people.

Amelia snorted with impatience.

"Did Zoey ever show any interest?" I asked, curious. "In licensing, I mean?"

"Not yet," Derek admitted. "But we're still in touch. Still talking."

Amelia rolled her eyes.

"I also represent fine artists to galleries," Derek said. "My business is about fifty-fifty."

"You're an artist agent in LA?" Tom said. "We've been told the dead man has or had a gallery there, maybe called Kendall's? Are you aware of it?"

Derek shook his head. "No." Then he reconsidered. "Maybe there used to be one? Before my time, really, but I vaguely remember something."

His response was punctuated by a lightning flash outside the small, third-floor window. I pressed my lips together, annoyed. If we had internet, we could check out the prior or current existence of this gallery in minutes. Life without the World Wide Web was interesting.

"I'm an artist in LA, too!" Amelia called from the bed.

Tom swung around toward her. "Did you know the man?"

"No."

He backed slowly out of the doorway. "Thanks. Sorry to disturb. Lock the door. I'm a cop, I have to say—"

"Don't worry. We will!" Amelia yelled after us, and I was sure they would.

"That was interesting," I said to Tom.

"Not really. They said they never talked to the guy."

I laughed. "You know what I mean."

"Is there anyone else up here?" he asked.

"The waiter, Jordan Thomas. He did serve Mr. Clarkson. And he's from LA. But I asked Jordan if he knew the man's name earlier, and he said no. There's no light coming from under his door. He's had a long, hard day and has to be up early to serve breakfast. Do you want to talk to him anyway?"

Tom glanced back over his shoulder and down the hallway. "We haven't reached the point of banging on doors and waking people up yet. Maybe later."

"Later? It must be eleven at least."

"Later than now," Tom answered, but at least he smiled. "Let's check to make sure his door is locked." We walked back down the hallway, and Tom rattled Jordan's door. "Good," he said when it didn't open. We turned around and started toward the stairs.

"How old is Zoey?" he asked. "I always thought she was our age."

"She is. Thirty-seven. Why?"

"Fifteen years. That's a long time to be in love with your college crush."

I'd been in love with my middle-school crush for twenty years, but I didn't remind Tom. No point in shoving it in his face. He had history. I had history. The important thing was the present.

When we reached the second floor, we went back and knocked on Dan Dawes's door.

"Come in!" he called. "About time."

"About time for what?" Tom stood in the doorway.

"Oh." We were not who he'd been expecting. "About time for some groom, best man, and groomsman hijinks," Dan answered. "But I'm guessing that's not why you two are here."

"No, sorry." Tom apologized as we entered the

room. "You know Julia. I'm her boyfriend, Tom."
He ran through the whole setup once again. He
was state police, trying to get background on the
deceased and so on. Tom's speech had improved
with every interview. Too bad this was the last one.

Dan's brown hair was shiny and wet. Perhaps he
had been in the shower. But he was wearing the
same plaid shorts, shirt, and sweater he'd had on
earlier that evening. Who takes a shower and puts
on the clothes they just removed?

"Do you know where Jamie and Pete are?" Dan
asked, mildly interested. He didn't say anything
about the dead man.

"Jamie's with Zoey," I answered. "And Pete—"

"Is doing an errand for me," Tom finished.
Though what Pete would have been doing with
the storm raging outside, I couldn't imagine.
"What about you?" Tom continued. "We stopped
by earlier, and I don't think you were here."

"I stepped outside," he said. "For some air."

"Outside?" I couldn't think of a more miserable
place.

"There's a little porch off the dining room, very
protected," Dan answered.

This was mostly true, though the way the wind
was blowing, someone who had gone out there
couldn't completely avoid getting wet. It explained his shiny hair. Belatedly, I noticed a dripping windbreaker hanging on the back of the desk
chair. "I went for a smoke," he confessed. "Filthy
habit. I'm addicted. Rain or shine. I thought you'd
be happier if I didn't indulge in the house."

A smoke? He'd been gone for at least half an hour.
Tom didn't say anything, though, so I followed
suit.

Dan smoothed a hand over his wet head and gestured for us to sit down, which we did, side by side on the bed. He'd used the desk in his room to set up a full bar. There were bottles of scotch, bourbon, gin, and vodka, mixers like tonic, seltzer, and bottled water, and a silver ice bucket.

Dan noticed me noticing. "Can I offer you a nightcap? I haven't found any ice, but I have everything else."

I desperately wanted to say yes. I'd worked at the cocktail party and during the clambake meal and therefore hadn't had anything to drink since the sip of champagne at the rehearsal in the afternoon. I wasn't sure stone-cold sober was the way to face the events of the night.

"No, thanks," Tom said. "We won't be long."

Dan took his place in the easy chair across from us. "I do remember the man, of course. It was creepy that it happened so soon after I met him. We chatted about nothing consequential. The usual small talk."

"His name?" Tom prompted.

"Kendall Clarkson, like I told Julia."

"Did Clarkson say anything about when he arrived in Maine or where he was staying in town?" I asked.

"No. I thought he'd arrived only recently, but I'm not sure if he said that or what gave me that impression." Dan rubbed his chin thoughtfully. "I assumed he was a member of Zoey's family. She grew up in California."

She had. But she didn't have any family there. I didn't say this.

"Did he say what he did for a living?" Tom asked.

"Something about an art gallery," Dan answered.

"I remember, I was surprised. I'd assumed he was retired."

Clarkson did look like he could be retired.

"You don't know the gallery? Maybe its name?" Tom asked.

"Sorry. I'd never heard of the gallery. My impression was that it was small. More in the nature of a hobby."

"Do you collect art?" I asked. He certainly was rich enough.

"I dabble," Dan said, "but I'm unaware of this gallery."

"Beside your family seated at the table, did anyone else come over to speak to Mr. Clarkson or otherwise come near him?" Tom asked.

Dan shook his head. "No. Just the waiter, like I told Julia earlier. That was it."

It didn't seem like there was anything more to say. Evidently, Dan felt the same because he rose from the chair. "When will Jamie and Pete be along?"

Tom and I stood as well. I was about to say, "Don't wait up," but Tom was faster. "Soon, I'm sure." With self-control, I didn't look at him in surprise.

"Why don't you lock your door while you wait, in case you drift off?" I suggested. It was an odd thing to say, but apparently not too odd. Dan nodded in response. "Roger that."

We stood in the hall until the lock tumbled. Then we walked to the landing. The storm had whipped up again. The wind wailed against the double-story window behind us, so loud we had to raise our voices to speak. At the same time, it felt like the wind and rain were also pummeling the front of the mansion, like the storm was coming from every direction all at once. Even from inside the house, I could hear the surf pounding against our dock. I was the one who was supposed to be used to storms on a small island, but I slipped my hand into Tom's for reassurance.

The door at the other end of the hallway opened, and Jamie came out of my apartment, closing it behind him. He advanced toward us. "I made Zoey tea," he said when he was close enough that we could hear him. "Constance is with her. I've come to check in."

"Great timing," Tom said. "We've just finished talking to everyone. Let's go down to the billiards room so we can bring you and Pete up to speed at the same time."

They stood aside so I could go first. My foot hovered over the top step, when down below, the front door flew open so fast it hit the wall behind it with a BANG! My breath caught, my knee buckled, and I began to tumble down the stairs.

CHAPTER TWELVE

A strong hand grabbed my shirt as I started to fall and hauled me back onto the landing. I was in Tom's arms while Jamie stared at us.

"Hello!" The call came from the foyer below.

My heart slowed, thumping so hard in my chest that I felt every beat. The voice belonged to my brother-in-law, Sonny. Of course, it did. We were on an island, and the sea was much too rough for anyone to arrive. It had to be someone who was already here.

"It's us," my sister, Livvie, called. Livvie and Sonny and their two kids stood dripping on the rug in the foyer below.

I hurried down to greet them and help them out of their sopping outerwear. "What are you doing here?" They were fully decked out in lobster-fishing gear—oilskin pants and jackets. Jack and Livvie wore headlamps. Sonny and Page carried heavy flashlights.

"The waves were crashing against the house," Livvie answered me.

"They almost came through the windows!" Six-year-old Jack's eyes burned with fear—and excitement.

The front of their house was set on pilings and stuck out over the Gulf of Maine. The front windows were at least ten feet above the waterline, even at high tide.

"We were scared. We saw the lights were still on up here, so we thought we'd come someplace a little safer," Livvie said.

Standing behind Livvie and Jack, water dripping from their identically colored bright red hair, Sonny and my niece, Page, wore the same expression. "Jack may have been scared," their faces said, "but don't lump us into that category."

"This place may not be safer." I said it under my breath. I intended it only for Livvie, but Sonny and Page heard and leaned forward with interest. "We have a few extra people here tonight," I informed them. "Why don't you stay in Mom's apartment?"

"Extra people?" Sonny asked. "Who in the world—"

Livvie seemed to understand this wasn't the time for a lengthy discussion. "Good idea. Let me get us settled in." She started for the stairs. "What the heck are you talking about?" she whispered as she walked by me. I shook my head hard, to indicate not to discuss it in front of the kids.

Sonny took another look, scanning across our faces—Jamie's, Tom's, and mine. "I'll come up with you," he said to Livvie. "To get you settled. Then I'll come down the get the story."

"I'll come up and walk you down," Jamie said. "We're using the buddy system tonight."

That earned a squint of inquiry from Sonny.

Livvie was already moving toward the stairs with the kids.

"Lock *both* doors," I reminded Sonny as he walked by me. My mother's apartment, carved out of the old master bedroom, dressing room, and study, had two doors, one out to the landing for the grand staircase, and one to a narrow set of stairs that in Windsholme's original design had led to the kitchen, allowing staff to come and go without being observed by family or guests.

Sonny nodded to show he understood. "Where will you be?"

"Billiards room."

When Tom and I got there, Pete, bored to death with no one to talk to but a corpse, was eager for news. We told him he'd have to wait until Sonny and Jamie arrived, which they did five minutes later. Sonny was toweling off his hair.

"What is going—whoa!" Sonny had spotted our unwanted guest. "What the what?"

Evidently, Jamie hadn't tipped Sonny off to anything. It was worth it to see his response.

"It's a long story," I answered. "We should all sit down."

Sonny fetched a dining chair from the main salon and joined the circle.

After we'd explained the dead man's continuing presence and our assumptions about the manner of his death, Sonny said, "Livvie's gonna want to hear this."

"I'll walk you up to stay with your kids and escort Livvie back here," Pete volunteered.

When Livvie arrived, we had to start all over again. She'd changed into a soft green sweatshirt and sweatpants that belonged to Mom, who was eight inches shorter. The sleeves fell just below Livvie's elbows and the pant legs just below her knees.

We told the beginning again, and then Tom and I went on to relate our conversations with the wedding party and our other guests, tag-team fashion.

"So let me get this straight," Livvie said when we were finished. "Neither Zoey nor Jamie knows this guy, but he was at the rehearsal dinner, yukking it up with the other guests like he belonged."

"And then he got himself murdered," Pete said. "Extreme behavior, even for a wedding crasher."

"We *think* he got himself murdered," Tom added for absolute accuracy.

"Right," I confirmed. "Did you talk to him at the cocktail party or the rehearsal dinner?"

"I was in the kitchen the whole time." Livvie stood up and went to look at the man. She studied him for several moments, head bent toward him, eyes intent. "I didn't see him at the cocktail party," she said, slowly. "But I'm sure I've seen him before."

"Where?" Tom asked. "When?"

"This week in Busman's Harbor," Livvie answered. "Tuesday, I think."

"Where, specifically?" Tom pressed.

Livvie drew in a deep breath and then said very quickly. "He was going into Lupine Design on Tuesday as I left work. Zoey let him in the studio door."

We were silent for a moment, all eyes on Jamie. Zoey had lied to all of us, but on the eve of their wedding, her lie to him felt like a particular betrayal. Why would she have done that? The Zoey I knew was honest and direct. It was a major reason our business partnership, and our friendship, worked.

We all shifted in our chairs. What to do next?

Livvie made the suggestion. "I think Julia and I should talk to Zoey, so she doesn't feel like she's being grilled by the police. No offense." She looked at Tom.

Jamie said, "I'm going with you." He didn't say more, but his face said it all. He was hurt and confused.

"Jamie," Livvie cautioned, "you're upset. There must be a reason Zoey claimed she didn't know the man. It's probably something embarrassing. It might be easier for her to tell us if you're not there."

"Or maybe I'm the only one she'll tell."

"She hasn't so far." Livvie let that statement sit there for a moment before she went on. "Let us try. If we don't get anywhere, then you can try. It's better to have more than one chance."

Jamie didn't react immediately, but then he gave a short wave of his hand to move the discussion along. He was giving in for the moment.

Tom looked at Livvie. "You're right. Zoey may be embarrassed if she's confronted. She's most likely to talk to you two."

When we got to my door, I was pleased to find it was locked. Constance let us in and read our expressions correctly. "I'll be in my room if I'm needed."

I wanted to urge her to get some sleep but didn't know what the night ahead held. I couldn't be sure we wouldn't want her to sit with Zoey again. I remained silent as she floated past us in the hallway and entered her room.

Zoey was still on the window seat, but she looked a little better. Her eyes were swollen, but not red, and the pile of used tissues by her side was much smaller. She had changed out of her rehearsal dress and wore a pair of pink pajamas. The bottoms were printed with graphics of bouquets and veils, rings, and white high heels. The T-shirt top had one word on it, "BRIDE!" It was the exclamation point that nearly broke my heart. This night was turning out so differently than she'd hoped.

Livvie went to Zoey immediately, kneeling by the window seat and taking her hand. "I am so sorry this happened."

Zoey waved a hand at the air, as if batting away a troublesome gnat. "No. I'm sorry. I'm being silly and selfish. It's just a wedding. Not even a wedding, a rehearsal dinner. That poor man is dead, and I'm fine. We're all fine." She gave me a tentative smile that seemed to ask for confirmation. *We are all fine.*

I smiled back, equally tentatively. "Honey," I said, "Livvie has something to ask you."

Livvie hesitated a moment, as if figuring out how to start, and then began. "Zoey, just now I saw the body of the man who died. I've seen him before. He came to the studio at closing time on Tuesday. Do you remember? You let him in."

Zoey's brows came together over her nose, a look of puzzlement—or consternation. "That was the same man?"

"Yes," Livvie said. "I'm sure."

Zoey was silent for a moment, thinking. "I remember now. He had some sort of business proposition. I told him he should talk to Julia in the morning." She looked at me. "Did he?"

"I'm certain I never saw him before today." I was very sure no one had come to me during the week with "some sort of business proposition." And if they had, I certainly would have told Zoey about it, even if I'd turned it down. Our partnership was built on the free flow of information. And, if it had happened that way, on any of the following days wouldn't Zoey have asked me if I'd spoken to the man? Both of us had been up to our eyebrows in wedding prep, and Zoey had been putting in massive hours at Lupine Design to complete her own work and provide instructions to the other potters so she could take off the time for her planned ten-day honeymoon. Maybe that explained the lapse. Still, I shifted uneasily, foot to foot.

Livvie squeezed Zoey's hand and looked into her eyes. "Zoey, honey, whatever it is, we'll understand. Everyone will understand."

"No." Zoey took her hand from Livvie and clasped it around her knees. Her whole body was turned inward on itself. She was shutting down. She was shutting us out.

I put a hand on Livvie's shoulder. I thought pushing Zoey might make things worse, diminishing the chances she would tell us whatever it was later.

"We have to go. There are still things to clear up." I said. "Should I get Constance?"

"No." Zoey didn't look at either of us. "I'm okay."

She obviously wasn't. "I'll be back as soon as I can," I assured her.

"Don't worry about it," Zoey swung her pajama-clad legs off the window seat. "I'm going to try to sleep."

"Lock the door," I reminded her. "I've got my key. If you're asleep, I can let myself in."

Livvie rose, after giving Zoey's shoulder a squeeze, and we made our way out the door.

"That was a complete failure," Livvie said after the lock had turned behind us.

"Yes," I agreed. "What could possibly be so important about this man that she won't tell us what she knows?"

"You don't think—" Livvie didn't finish the sentence.

Not without her reasons, Zoey had something the three of us jokingly called her "daddy issues." That explained the man she'd had an affair with before Jamie. He was twenty years older and not quite divorced. But Mr. Clarkson? I tried to imagine them together romantically and stopped with a shudder. "She invited at least one other ex," I said.

Livvie and I looked at each other in complete agreement. "No," we both said at the same time. "No."

On the landing outside Mom's apartment, Livvie said good night and went to be with her kids. "I'll send Sonny out to walk you down."

Tom, Pete, and Jamie were in the billiards room when Sonny and I entered. I told the group what Zoey had said, not bothering to hide my skepticism that it was the whole truth. I wasn't going to accuse Zoey of lying, especially in front of her fiancé. I had only a feeling to go on.

As it was, Jamie paced around the room like a caged animal, his fists clenched at his sides. He needed to do something, anything. His face betrayed his anger and his helplessness.

Zoey was an honest person, but she wasn't beyond having secrets. She'd spent her growing-up years keeping her own counsel, hiding the chaos of life with her mother from teachers, friends, and their well-meaning parents. After her mother was murdered by a boyfriend, Zoey had soldiered on, keeping most of her former life secret. She'd had to tell Derek, because he'd been her boyfriend during the trial, which had been highly publicized. Besides, he'd been her lover at the time.

But so was Jamie. He was her lover, soon to be her husband, and the father of their child. I couldn't imagine what would cause Zoey to lie to him. Something big. Huge. That she could barely admit to herself.

I knew Jamie and Zoey well and had faith in them as a couple. I was sure Zoey would come clean to Jamie soon. Otherwise, it wouldn't be a good way to start married life. My ex, Chris Durand, had been a five-star keeper of secrets, so I knew how it felt when they were finally revealed. Terrible.

"I'm going to talk to her," Jamie said.

We couldn't tell him not to. He was her fiancé. The only hope was persuasion. "Give her some time," I urged him. "She's trying to rest." I looked at Tom and said as calmly as I could, "I think it would be better if we waited until we had more information to share with her, and therefore more reason to go back and ask again." Zoey was trapped in a disintegrating lie. We had to find a way to lead her out of it.

We'd been talking to people all evening and knew little more than we had known from the moment Tom had found Kendall Clarkson's wallet.

"Is it time to tell the other guests this man was murdered," Pete asked, "for their own protection?"

Tom shrugged his shoulders, the muscles rippling under his shirt, and then looked at the back of his hands. His cop's instinct was to keep his cards as close to his chest as possible. But that was warring with his duty to keep everyone in the house safe. "We have no reason to believe the killer is here. Numbers alone suggest that whoever it was went back on the tour boat."

"We've told them all to lock their doors," I pointed out.

"Which won't prevent them from opening them when someone knocks," Pete argued. "You've just proved that."

"Okay." Tom gave in. "But we need to get something out of the disclosure. We'll question the guests again to see if knowing the man was murdered knocks anything loose." He paused. "Jamie and Pete, you talk to Dan Dawes. Maybe a friendly face will jog his memory. Julia and I will talk to Constance Marshall and then Bill Lascelle. Each of them was holding something back. Sonny, are you okay to stay with Mr. Clarkson?"

"He's safe with me."

"Are you sure you want to be here on your own?" I was certain Sonny could take care of himself, but I felt I had to ask on Livvie's behalf.

"Don't worry about me." Sonny crossed his arms over his chest. "I'll be right here."

CHAPTER THIRTEEN

Constance answered her door still wearing the pale blue terry-cloth robe. "I hoped you'd come back," she said. "With the phones out, I had no way to reach you without wandering the halls on a stormy night."

"You were smart to stay put." Tom walked into her room, and I followed. "Have you remembered something?"

"More like decided to come clean about something."

Tom cocked an eyebrow. "Oh."

We sat in our previous places, Tom in the desk chair, me on the bed, and Constance in the leather easy chair. "But did you come to tell me something?" she asked.

"You first," Tom shot back.

She settled herself, shifting a little and pressing her hands together as if in prayer, but then placed her clasped hands in her lap. "I wasn't entirely honest with you before." She wiggled again, her physical discomfort mirroring something going on inside. "Many years ago, I lived with a man who told me his name was Kenneth Clark." She responded to Tom's raised eyebrows by hurrying onward. "It lasted several months, then we broke up."

"Kenneth Clark," I clarified. "Not Kendall Clarkson."

"He was the same man." Constance said it without hesitation.

"The nature of your relationship was—" Tom suggested.

"Romantic," Constance said. "We were lovers."

"How long ago was this?' Tom asked.

Constance cast her eyes heavenward, remembering or calculating. "Nearly forty years."

"Why did you break up?" I asked.

"The usual reasons. We weren't made for the long haul."

"Have you seen each other since?" I wanted to know. "Maybe through Zoey?" He was clearly something to Zoey.

"I haven't seen him from that day to this. When I spotted him at the cocktail hour, you could have knocked me over with a feather. I mean that literally. It would have taken very little. I felt like I was going to fall down anyway. I had no idea he was going to be here. I didn't think he had any connection to Zoey, who wasn't born when he and I were together." She closed her eyes for a second and then opened them again. They were enormous and truly gray, not the light blue people sometimes called gray. "But Zoey says she doesn't know him either. Have you found out why he was here?"

Constance hadn't been in the room the second

time we talked with Zoey and didn't know that Zoey had admitted to meeting the man.

"Not as yet," Tom answered. "When you and Mr. Clark or Clarkson were together, did he tell you anything about his connections? Children, siblings, nieces, nephews, anyone who should be notified of his death?"

Constance didn't hesitate. "Never. He didn't have children. At least not then. I understood he was estranged from his family." She paused and then added, "I believe Clark may be his original name, in case you find that helpful."

"Yes, thanks, we may," Tom responded. "You've already said you talked to him at the party. Your conversation with him seemed heated, at least on your side. That doesn't seem like a reaction to an amicable parting forty years ago. What upset you?"

Constance hung her head. "You'll think I'm silly." She spoke into her lap. "He didn't recognize me." A bright red blush crept up the white skin of her neck. When she lifted her head, her cheeks were blazing. She cleared her throat, a delicate ethem. "When I spotted him at the cocktail party, I walked up to him and asked how he was, like a civilized person. I had the next question planned out in my head: how did he know Zoey, or Jamie, but I never got to it. He put his hand out and said his name, 'Kendall Clarkson,' like we'd never met. I wasn't fooled. I said to him, 'Ken. It's Constance. Marshall. We lived together for eight months.' He looked at me and said, 'I'm certain not.'

"I know I've aged, but then so had he, and I recognized him instantly. I thought, even if I look different, once I tell him my name, he'll make the connection. But he continued to stare at me like he'd never seen me in his life. 'You are mistaken, madam,' he said, all formal. Then he tried to make a joke. 'You must have lived with my doppelgänger.'

"I said, 'Cut the crap, Ken.' I was furious. 'I know it's been some years, but I will not have my history erased. I don't care what you're calling yourself now. You may have a new name, but that doesn't mean you have a new history.'" Constance stopped talking and breathed in heavily through her nose. "Sorry."

"Don't apologize." I imagined running into Chris on some day far in the future and having him look right through me, claiming all we had, all we went through never existed. I would be furious, too.

"As I understand you," Tom said, bringing us back to the task at hand, "when you lived with him, the man was Ken Clark. Today he told you his name was Kendall Clarkson, correct?"

Constance nodded.

"You told us the name was Kendall Clarkson when we spoke to you earlier." It was a statement of fact. There was no accusation in Tom's tone.

"I didn't intend to tell you any of this. Giving you the name he was currently using made more sense in the circumstances."

"And you weren't going to tell us because—" Tom asked.

"I find it embarrassing," Constance said, though she seemed a little more self-assured than she had earlier. "At the time, you were looking for his identity and next of kin. I have no idea about the next of kin, and it seemed to me what I knew about his identity would only add to the confusion."

"You didn't chat with Mr. Clarkson tonight about showing your artwork in his gallery," I said.

Constance shook her head. "No. That was a summation of the first conversation we ever had when we met at the original Getty Museum forty years ago."

We all sat for a moment in silence.

"Is there anything else you've failed to tell us?" Tom asked, not unkindly.

"No!" Constance was vehement.

"Thank you," Tom said.

"But why did you come here in the first place?" Constance asked.

Tom sat forward in the wooden chair, almost resting on his haunches. "I am sorry to tell you that we believe the man you knew as Ken Clark was murdered."

Constance's mouth dropped open. "How?" she asked. I could have sworn she was surprised, shocked even. But I hadn't spotted that she was lying earlier when Tom had.

"I'm sorry, but I can't disclose that at this time," Tom answered.

"Why?" She stuttered the word out. "Who?"

Tom brushed nonexistent crumbs off his pants. "We don't know. I don't suppose you'd have any idea?"

"I told you I hadn't seen him in forty years." Constance had got control of her voice.

Tom stood. "It appears the murder was planned and targeted. However, we're asking everyone to keep their door locked. Don't let anyone in unless it's Julia, or me, Jamie, or Pete," he added.

"Certainly." Constance seemed herself again.

Out in the hall, we listened for the sound of the

lock. I wondered if I would ever feel the same way about that modest household sound again. "Where now?" I asked Tom.

Jamie and Pete came out of Dan Dawes's room. We moved to the second-floor landing, where we had a hurried, whispered conversation.

"Did your nephew tell you anything?" Tom's tone indicated interest, but not expectation.

"No," Jamie said, and behind him, Pete shook his head. "Nothing beyond what he told you. He was sitting next to the victim when he keeled over. They had traded pleasantries, nothing more." Jamie spread his fingers out, looking down at the backs of his hands. "He's family." Jamie opened his mouth and then closed it again and left it at that.

Tom picked up on that immediately. "You thought there was more he wasn't saying?"

Behind Jamie, Pete was rigorously shaking his head up and down.

"Yes," Jamie said, his voice even lower than the whisper we'd been conversing in. "We've been close all our lives, and he's my groomsman. I think you'd get more out of him than we did." That was a lot for Jamie to admit.

"He may not have told you anything more because there was nothing to tell," Tom said, ignoring Pete. "I want to talk to Lascelle before we double up on anyone. You told Dan it was murder, right?" Jamie and Pete nodded. "Good. Why don't you two talk to the waiter next?"

Jamie and Pete headed for Jordan's room on the third floor, while Tom and I knocked on Bill Lascelle's door.

Lascelle was still awake and dressed. He let us in
with a look of mild inquiry but remained standing.
Tom went through his spiel about possible murder, obviously need to know more, et cetera.

"Of course," Lascelle said, "but I've told you all I
know."

"Why don't you take me through the entire conversation you had with Kendall Clarkson," Tom
suggested, "sentence by sentence, word by word."

Lascelle stepped back, not exactly staggering,
but clearly considering his options. He was quiet
for a long time. In the end, he must have concluded that he couldn't sustain a lie over the length
of making up an entire conversation. "You'd better sit down. This is going to take a while, though I
doubt you'll find it valuable."

We sat, and so did he. "I wasn't entirely open before. I did know the man you tell me is dead, murdered. I didn't think what I knew would be at all
helpful in discovering his next of kin, or whatever
you told me your mission was before, so I kept it to
myself."

"Now that it's suspected murder," Tom said,
"everything matters."

"Indeed." Lascelle cleared his throat and began.
"A decade ago, I was persuaded to exhibit several
pieces at Clarkson's gallery. I was initially skeptical.
I'd never heard of Clarkson, and no one else I
talked to had either. But his gallery was a beautiful
space in the Arts District in LA. My work would
look amazing in it. I had newly signed with an
agent, who had gotten me the gig and was wildly
enthusiastic. I wanted to keep him onside. I had a
reputation in the community and a successful pot-

tery business, much like Zoey's. This was to be my first foray into the fine art market.

"The show was, to all appearances, a success. On opening night, there were little 'sold' stickers by every piece. Everyone who was anyone was there. There were lots of rich buyers and press. I was overjoyed."

He shifted in the chair. "But when my agent approached Clarkson for payment, nothing was forthcoming. At first, Clarkson said he was waiting for people to arrange to pick up their pieces and pay him. Then he said the money was tied up in some kind of bureaucratic tangle; there was sales tax to be paid and so on. I knew I wouldn't be getting all the money. The gallery and the tax man and my agent would get their cuts, but the amount that would come to me was meaningful. Maybe not materially—my commercial business was very successful by then—but in validation of my work and the direction I was taking.

"It became clear, eventually, that no money was coming. I flew to Los Angeles and drove to the gallery myself. All I found was an empty loft. No one could find Kendall Clarkson or the gallery. I never got paid.

"When I saw Clarkson at the party tonight, I was surprised, to say the least. I never knew he had any connection to Zoey. I didn't approach him at first. I couldn't think of what to say. I was angry. He had disappeared with my money. But it was ten years ago. I'd long ago given up on the money and decided to forget about the whole incident. Lesson learned.

"When I did finally approach him at the cocktail party, he didn't acknowledge we had previously met.

We started chatting comfortably enough. Why are you here, who do you know, and so on. I said I was an old friend of Zoey's and would be playing guitar at the wedding."

"What did he say?" Tom asked.

"I remember because the way he expressed it was slightly odd. He said the bride had invited him. Not that he was a friend of Zoey's. I know she doesn't have any relatives. But that she had asked him to come."

"And the conversation from there?" Tom prompted.

"I couldn't let it go. I did bring up the money. I said, 'I haven't forgotten what you owe me.'"

"How did he react?" I asked, fascinated.

"He claimed he didn't remember me. Or the show. Or my work."

"Did you think he was lying?" I asked. "Or, in your opinion, had he genuinely forgotten?"

"I could see he might have forgotten me. We only met three times. When I staged the work for the show, at the opening, when I came by the next day, floating on air because everything had sold. Ha! But he couldn't have forgotten the show. Or my agent bugging him twice a week for payment for months."

"What is the name of your agent?" I asked.

"Derek Quinn was representing me at the time. We've parted ways since."

Derek Quinn, who was currently upstairs in a bedroom with his girlfriend.

"Did the nonpayment from the victim contribute to your breakup with Mr. Quinn?" Tom asked.

"The vic—" Lascelle's brow furrowed, but then

cleared. He smiled. His teeth were crowded on the bottom, and one of the front ones stuck out slightly. "I always think of myself as the victim," he said. "The mess with Clarkson may have contributed to my leaving Derek, but it certainly wasn't the only reason. The break didn't come until two years later, in any case."

Bill put his elbows on his knees and steepled his hands together. "Derek was pretty green when I went with him. I'd always represented myself, but he had great contacts in the industry for licensing my work on the commercial side. For the fine-art thing, the truth is we were both inexperienced and probably naïve. I listened to Derek even when my gut told me not to. I shouldn't have."

"Have you spoken with Mr. Quinn about Mr. Clarkson at any time today?" Tom asked.

"I haven't spoken to Derek at all. I was surprised he was here. I had no idea he and Zoey had kept in touch. He was firmly in her past by the time she worked for me. And tonight, he stayed close to Zoey, from what I observed. I didn't want to enter that scrum."

"Is there anything else you haven't told me?" Tom asked.

"Absolutely nothing," Lascelle said.

"Thanks." Tom stood, and so did I. "You see the importance of locking your door," he added.

Lascelle rose and then saluted. "Aye, aye, sir. You'll have noticed it was locked when you came along this time."

"I did, and I appreciate it," Tom said, and we left.

CHAPTER FOURTEEN

"Were they telling the truth this time?" I asked Tom as we walked down the hall. "Constance and Bill?

"We're getting closer to it."

I was fascinated. I'd helped Tom with investigations before, but I'd never had a chance to watch him question witnesses.

We had another hurried discussion with Jamie and Pete on the landing. They were there, waiting, when Tom and I came out of Lascelle's room.

"Anything?" Tom asked.

"We woke the kid out of a sound sleep. When we told him we were cops, he was terrified—and barely coherent after that. When we told him the man was murdered, I thought he was going to levitate off the bed. I hated to leave him, to tell the truth; he was so freaked out."

"One interesting thing," Pete added. "His mother was here tonight. Works for the caterer."

His mother. She had to be the woman Carol Trevett had said was named Mel. I squinted, trying to see if there was a resemblance. They were both tall, but he was lanky and loose-jointed, while she had been rigid, ramrod straight. Her hair was dark, almost black, and his was sandy. Maybe there was something around the eyes? The bigger question was, why hadn't Jordan mentioned this, or introduced his mother when they came off the boat or when I found him talking to the caterers in the kitchen? He was young and shy, and maybe he'd forgotten his manners.

"What about Lascelle?" Pete asked.

"It turns out he did know the victim from before," Tom told him. "And Clarkson owed Lascelle money. From a gallery show where allegedly all the pieces were sold, but Lascelle and his agent were never paid."

"His agent was Derek Quinn." I added.

"All these people are connected," Jamie said.

"Not unusual at a wedding," I responded. "These are Zoey's friends."

"Except the victim," Jamie reminded us. "She'd met him once, last Tuesday."

"What's next?" Pete asked.

"We're going to talk to Derek Quinn," Tom told them. "If Clarkson owed Lascelle money, he owed Quinn, too. Why don't you two go down and check on Sonny?"

Jamie gave a longing look at the closed door of my apartment at the other end of the hall. No light showed from under the door, but that didn't mean there wasn't one on in the separate bedroom. I hoped Zoey was asleep, even though that meant we'd undoubtedly have to wake her at some point.

Jamie turned back, and he and Pete clattered down the staircase.

"Would you invite Chris to our wedding?" Tom asked as we climbed the stairs to the third floor.

"Are we having a wedding?" I kept my tone light.

"This is a theoretical question."

"Then, no," I answered. "We didn't have time after we broke up to become real friends." I hesitated. "I think we were in a good place when he moved to Florida, but we haven't communicated since, so I wouldn't say we were friends." In a weird way, Chris and I had grown into adulthood together, and I would always love him, or at least the memory of him. But no.

"Glad to hear it," Tom said.

"You're not in a position to ask me that," I countered. "Given that your ex-fiancée is now married to your brother. She'll have to be at this theoretical wedding."

"Now you see why I avoid family gatherings."

"But you won't forever."

My family was a magnet for strays, people with no other family who joined the circle. Chris had been one, the captain another. So was Zoey, though now she was gaining a huge family through Jamie. But I didn't think of Tom as a stray, and I didn't want him to be. I knew he talked to his mom at least once a week. He wouldn't stay outside their circle much longer.

I didn't think anything of the "theoretical wedding" conversation. It was a game most couples who'd been together for a while played. Chris and I had played it, and we'd never had a wedding.

We were outside Derek and Amelia's door by this point. Amelia answered immediately when Tom knocked. "It's you," she said, stepping back, clearly not happy to see us. She was wearing the Snowden Family Clambake T-shirt, which fell to mid-thigh.

"Were you expecting someone else?" Tom asked.

"No. Just hoping." Amelia turned away and flounced toward the bed. Derek was the one in it this time, sheet pulled decorously to his waist. "Why are you here? It's almost midnight."

Tom stepped inside the room, and I followed, closing the door behind us. "We're back because we have news," he said. "The man who we presumed had an allergic attack earlier, we now have indications that he may have been murdered."

Tom stopped talking while Derek and Amelia made appropriately shocked noises. Derek's mouth hung open, and he breathed heavily, in and out. He looked like a landed fish. Amelia looked more puzzled than surprised, even as she was demanding to know what had happened and how we planned to protect them.

"That's why we're telling you this," Tom explained patiently. "So you're aware and can protect yourselves. Keep the door locked, and don't answer it unless it's me, Julia, Jamie, or Pete Howland on the other side. I told you before I was with the state police. To be more specific, I'm a detective with the Major Crimes Unit."

"You're a what?" Amelia blinked.

"A Maine State—"

"I heard," she interrupted. "I just couldn't believe it. You don't seem smart enough."

Tom ignored her. He'd heard worse insults, I was sure.

"How?" Derek asked. "How was he murdered?"

"We can't be sure of anything yet, without a postmortem," Tom turned to Derek. "Mr. Quinn," Tom began, all the informality of the previous conversation dropping away, "Bill Lascelle has told us you were his agent some time ago. And that you and he did business with Kendall Clarkson. Yet you denied it when I asked you if you knew him. You denied knowing that he owned a gallery."

Derek swung his legs out of the bed. Apparently, this wasn't a conversation he wanted to have lying down. I turned away as he shrugged into his shorts and caught a glimpse of Amelia's wide-eyed expression. She hadn't known about Derek's association with Clarkson either.

Derek came closer, and we all remained standing. "It was years ago. It had nothing to do with tonight. I thought it would just confuse things."

"We're not so easily confused." Tom didn't like Derek, I could tell, but he remained professional. If Tom had been rude to the guy, it would have been because he thought it would get him what he needed. "According to Bill Lascelle, Clarkson stiffed you both," Tom continued. "Maybe that gives you a motive?"

"Look, man," Derek said, "when you asked before, I didn't know it was murder. You didn't ask me if I had a motive to kill him. You asked who he was. I figured there were a lot of other people around here who could tell you."

"Like Bill Lascelle," I suggested.

"Like Zoey," Amelia countered. "Obviously, she must have invited him."

Tom cut in quickly. "Why don't you tell us what happened with Mr. Clarkson, Derek. We've already heard what Bill Lascelle has to say."

Derek did sit down, suddenly, on the bed, like his legs had gone to jelly. "I'm sure it will be the same story because it happened to both of us, although Bill blamed me. He was right. I saw this big opportunity for him—and for me—and I ignored the red flags."

"Which were?" Tom asked.

"The gallery was new. When I asked Clarkson about other artists who had shown there and what sales were like, he was vague, very, very vague. But he was smooth as glass. He seemed to know everyone. The opening night was amazing. I've never seen so many rich people in one place from that day to this. The arts press covered it. I thought we'd hit the big time.

"But Clarkson didn't pay us. I nagged him politely and then less politely. Bill was on my back every day. Clarkson stopped answering my calls. Then his number was no longer in service, and his emails bounced. I went to the gallery, but it was gone."

"Did you go to the police?" Tom asked.

"I did. They couldn't find Clarkson either, though apparently they knew who he was. He'd already been in jail a few times for similar stuff."

"And that's the last you saw of Mr. Clarkson until tonight?" Tom asked.

"Yes," Derek answered. "Five years after all that happened, an FBI agent came to see me. The feds had Clarkson by that point. He was in prison for something else. The charges they had Clarkson on, which I think were forgery, weren't going to keep him in prison long. They wanted more. The agent asked me the same questions I'd answered five years earlier. I never heard from him or anyone else again."

"Do you remember the agent's name or what field office he was out of?"

"No." Derek shrugged.

"Do you know if this FBI agent talked to Lascelle?" Tom asked.

"No idea."

"How much did Clarkson steal from you?" I had no idea how much it would be.

"Every piece in the room sold. Bill and I would have netted about a hundred thousand dollars."

A lot of money.

Tom squared his shoulders and stared down at Derek. "You can see why we need to know anything, anything at all, that you heard or observed at the party, on the boat, any time."

"Nothing." Amelia answered instead of Derek. "I never saw him before tonight. And I'm not sure I saw him even then. You were all crowded around him when he fell over, and then you hauled him off somewhere."

Derek, however, was quiet, staring down at his lap. "I didn't see the man or speak to him at the rehearsal dinner," he said slowly. "But I have seen him this week, since we got to Busman's Harbor."

I stared at him, startled by the admission.

"Tell us when and where," Tom said.

Derek nodded and sat up straighter. "We've been here for a week. We figured if we were going to come all the way east for the wedding, we'd make a vacation of it. The first day we were here, Tuesday, I went along to let Zoey know we were in town."

Amelia's sharp glance at her boyfriend told me she was hearing this for the first time. It had been a night of revelations for her.

"When I arrived at the shop, I went to the studio door, hoping to catch Zoey alone." This drew a venomous look from Amelia. "As I came around the corner, Zoey was letting Clarkson out." Derek stopped talking, but he wasn't done. I could feel the three of us holding our breath. "She hugged him good-bye. She was crying. I turned around and left. I didn't want to disturb her."

"You're sure it was Clarkson?" Tom kept his voice even.

Derek shrugged. "Yes. I almost had a heart attack when I recognized him."

Who else would it have been? Livvie had already told us the dead man was at Lupine Design on Tuesday. And Zoey crying when he left was a pretty clear indication it hadn't been a conversation about a business opportunity.

Tom shifted his weight forward, ready to turn around and depart. "Thanks. Don't forget about the door," he told them when we reached it. But Amelia had followed behind us and was already swinging the old oak door shut.

"He's a liar!"

Jamie didn't take the news well. Tom told him, in a calm, low voice, that Derek Quinn claimed to have seen Clarkson leaving Lupine Design—and Zoey in tears—on Tuesday in the late afternoon.

Pete and Sonny had been sound asleep in the satiny chairs in the billiards room, heads thrown back, mouths open and snoring, when Tom and I had entered. Jamie had been on his feet, pacing, fists clenched, ready to hit someone. And that was before we told him what Derek had said.

"Whut?" Sonny came to, blinking, awakened by Jamie's shout. Pete woke up, too.

Someone had fetched a sheet and draped it over the body. It was seemlier to have Mr. Clarkson covered, but I vowed to take the sheet to our firepit and burn it as soon as it was removed.

"It's obvious Quinn killed this guy." Jamie gestured toward the sheet. "Now he's trying to set Zoey up to take the blame."

The words, "But Derek loves Zoey!" almost burst out of me, but I restrained myself at the last moment.

"Let's take a breath, sit down, and figure out what we know and what to do next." Tom, leading by example, sat, and I did, too. Jamie looked around, made a gesture of submission, and fetched another chair from the main salon.

"We'll start at the beginning," Tom said. "A man is dead, quite possibly—no, probably—he was murdered. He has an injection mark behind his left ear."

Everyone nodded their agreement.

"His name, at least currently, is Kendall Clarkson. He may earlier have called himself Kenneth Clark, according to Constance Marshall. She had a relationship with the dead man forty years ago."

"Is that a motive?" Sonny asked.

"It happened decades ago," I answered. "She doesn't seem to have had a terrible life or anything. Just the opposite, according to Zoey. Why would she hold on to a resentment that long?" I paused, thinking. "She was angry because he didn't recognize her at the cocktail party."

"This murder was the opposite of spontaneous," Tom reminded us. "Whoever did it had to bring the poison and syringe. Ms. Marshall claims she didn't know the victim would be here. She didn't know he had any connection to Zoey."

"He didn't have any connection to Zoey," Jamie objected.

The rest of us ignored him, and the conversation moved forward.

"Which brings us to Quinn himself." I sensed Tom had led the discussion to Derek Quinn next to keep Jamie from imploding. "He had an old association with the dead man, which he concealed. And the dead man owed him money."

"Not that much money," I pointed out. "What would the agent's share of a hundred thousand dollars be? And it was over ten years ago. Would you murder someone for a negligible debt, one you'd more than recovered from, that far in the past? Bill Lascelle lost a lot more."

"We'll get to him," Tom said. "Also, Quinn knew Clarkson was in town." He held a hand up in Jamie's direction to stop the expected protestation. "Quinn says he saw him at Zoey's studio on Tuesday. He could have reasonably concluded Clarkson would be here tonight, or at least hoped he would."

"I don't see it," Pete said. "It's a stretch. If Zoey was crying when Clarkson left, why would Quinn assume he was invited to the wedding?"

"Unless we don't know the whole story." Jamie was practically horizontal in his chair, arms folded across his chest.

"Mr. Lascelle," Tom continued, "he also initially concealed his association with Clarkson. He also lost money. More money than Quinn, as Julia says."

"Same issues," I said. "It was a long time ago. Bill's a successful businessman. It may have been a material amount of money at the time, but is it now? Besides, we have no indication he knew Clarkson would be here."

"Could Lascelle and Quinn have done it together?" Sonny had been listening right along but hadn't spoken. He hadn't done any of the interviews and didn't really know the players.

"Those guys can't stand each other," Tom said. "Makes it hard to believe."

"Could that be an act?" Pete asked.

"I don't think so," I answered. "I think they really hate each other."

"Something more than a business deal gone bad," Sonny suggested.

"Maybe." Tom said the word slowly, considering.

"Where does that leave us?" Pete asked.

Head down, Tom looked at Jamie from under his eyebrows. "We need to get Zoey to tell us what's really going on."

That brought Jamie to his feet. "No way!"

"Jamie—" I started.

"She's exhausted. Her wedding is ruined. She's been planning it for so long. She's worn out and disappointed."

And pregnant. I didn't say it.

"Think about it," Jamie continued. "Would she destroy her own wedding by killing this guy, whoever he is to her?"

And your wedding, too. As hard as he was working to protect Zoey, Jamie had to be feeling all those emotions as well. He'd dreamed of marriage and a family for years.

"We could all give up and go to bed," Sonny suggested. "Things might look different in the morning."

"That's just it," Tom said. "Things will be different in the morning. The storm will be over, and at some point, the phones and internet will return. Or one of us will go to town to call my office. Professionals will be arriving, lots of them. If Zoey keeps lying, it will be bad for her." He stared directly at Jamie. "We should try, one more time, to persuade her to tell the truth. For her own sake."

The room was silent as we digested this.

"I'm coming with you," Jamie said.

It didn't seem like a good idea, but Tom didn't argue. The three of us stood and moved toward the door.

CHAPTER FIFTEEN

There was no light seeping from under my apartment door. I unlocked it and pushed the door
open. "Zoey?" I called very softly. "You asleep?"

Once we were in the main room, I could see a
light coming from the bedroom beyond. Either
Zoey was sleeping with the light on, or she was up.
"I'm going to check on her," I whispered to the
guys. "You stay here."

Jamie didn't argue, which surprised me.

Zoey was sitting up in my bed. She had her enormous wedding planner notebook open on her lap.
She'd obviously been turning the pages, indulging
in nostalgia for her fantasy wedding. Whatever she
thought was happening tomorrow, it wouldn't be
the magical wedding contained in those pages.

"Julia, at last. Do you think the storm is slowing
down? If it stops soon, everything will be fine by
the time the guests get here, don't you think? The
sun will dry the grass."

"I do think the storm is passing." I sat next to

her on the bed. "Honey, Jamie and Tom are here. Tom has more questions about the man."

I expected a fight, but Zoey put the notebook to the side and pulled her knees toward her, ready to climb out of the bed. "Let's get this over with. I want this—" she groped for the right word. I thought of several, none of them worth suggesting—disaster, tragedy, unreal, unexpected outrage. "Thing," she finally labeled it, "over and done with before to-morrow morning."

I went to my closet and handed her my worn flannel robe to put over the pink bride pajamas.

"Thanks." She ran her fingers through her curly brown hair, wilder now than it was in the daytime. A hairdresser was arriving on the first run of the Boston Whaler in the morning. Darn. Another thing I'd have to cancel.

Jamie and Tom had turned on the lights and were seated at my kitchen table. Zoey went over, gave Jamie a kiss on his forehead and sat down. I sat, too. Jamie took Zoey's hand.

Tom began. "Zoey, we need to ask you some more questions about the dead man and your meeting with him."

Her eyes opened wider. They were still a bit swollen. "Has something else happened?"

Tom spread his hands out on the table, as if placing his cards face up. "Yes and no. I need you to take me back through your meeting with him on Tuesday."

"I told you everything I could. The man came by the studio just as we were closing."

"What time was that?"

"Four o'clock."

Tom nodded for Zoey to go on.

"He said his name was Kendall Clarkson. He wanted to pitch a business deal. I told him to come back Wednesday morning when I knew Julia would be in the office. End of story."

She paused and looked at each of us in turn. Tom was stone-faced. Jamie's lips formed a tight, straight line. He closed his fists on the white table-top, ready to defend anything Zoey might say. It must have been my face that gave it away.

"Oh," Zoey said. "You know."

Tom replaced his emotionless expression with one of openness and kindness. "We don't know, Zoey. But Derek Quinn told us he came to see you around five on Tuesday. He saw Clarkson leaving your studio, and he saw you crying when the man left. A discussion of a business deal, quickly deflected, doesn't take an hour. It doesn't elicit the level of emotion Quinn saw, either."

"*Claims* he saw," Jamie corrected.

"Claims he saw," Tom confirmed.

Zoey didn't say anything for a long time. Then she looked at Jamie. Tears ran from the corners of her eyes, making tracks down her cheeks and landing on my ratty bathrobe. "He came to the studio on Tuesday with no warning. I had never seen him before in my life. He's my father."

She put her head down on the table, cradled it in her arms, and sobbed as if her heart were broken.

For a moment, Tom, Jamie, and I were absolutely still, stunned into inaction. Jamie recovered first. He leaned over and pulled Zoey onto his lap. She buried her face in his shirt and went on crying.

I looked at Tom. Could we stop asking questions? It seemed cruel to go on, but also wrong to leave, having caused so much upheaval. Maybe Zoey would want to talk once she calmed down.

I wondered how life could be so unfair. Zoey's mother had been murdered when she was a teenager. Was it possible her father had been murdered too, twenty years later and on the other side of the country? It seemed so improbable.

I went to fetch a box of tissues. By the time I came back, Zoey had stopped crying and was making little hiccupping noises. At last, she pulled her head off Jamie's shoulder. He still held onto her like he couldn't let her go.

"Zoey—" I started.

"I know," she said. She wiped her eyes and blew her nose. I pulled the kitchen trash bucket out and offered it up to her. She spiked the tissue hard. She was angry as well as sad. Of course, she was.

"Can you take us back through that afternoon?" Tom asked softly.

She could have said no, but she didn't. "Okay." She got off Jamie's lap and moved back to her chair so she could look at all of us as she spoke. "I'm ready."

We were looking at her, wondering what she would say.

"My mother told me nothing about my father. The man. His name isn't on my birth certificate. Whenever I asked, she told me my father was in prison, where I wouldn't be able to visit.

"But even though Mom wouldn't talk about *who* he was, she did tell me their story. She wanted me to know 'I came from love.' My mother was a romantic. And she had an unfortunate attraction to terrible men. I knew both of these things about her from an early age. I didn't have a fantasy that my dad was a great guy who would reenter my life and rescue me. But I did want to know about him. I wanted to know if my nose came from him, or my body type, so different from my mother's. I loved her stories and encouraged her to tell them as often as possible."

Tom shifted in his seat, eager to get on to the part about the stranger in the billiards room downstairs but too experienced to rush her. Jamie was still apparently content to wait. I was dying to hear it all.

"They met at a concert, an outdoor concert. Sometimes she said it was the Dead, but I think that was to make it sound cooler. Whatever it was, Mom was sitting with a friend on a blanket, and this man, this very handsome man, swaggered by and stepped on the blanket."

Kendall Clarkson had been a handsome man. He'd cut a fine figure as he'd moved through the crowd at the cocktail party with his thick, white hair, white mustache, and warm brown eyes. Did I see any of him in Zoey? My imagination couldn't bridge the differences in age and gender.

"Mom called the man out about stepping on the blanket," Zoey was saying. "He apologized. A conversation started. Mom always said it was love at first sight. She was in art school; he was an artist, too. At the end of the concert, she brought him back to the apartment where she lived with a roommate. He said on that very first day that she was the most beautiful woman he'd ever known and that he was hopelessly in love with her.

"They spent the summer together, going out to hear music, staying in and painting each other. He painted my mother in the nude. I remember the picture. It hung in our various apartments for many years, until my mother's last boyfriend—" Zoey's voice wavered. Her mother's last boyfriend had killed her. "He didn't like the painting, or that a former lover had painted it. My mother took it down and put it in a closet. When I went into foster care, it was lost."

A terrible loss. An image of her mother, created by her father.

"I'm sorry," Tom said, his voice low and encouraging. "But the man downstairs—"

"He came to my studio, like I told you. I took him out front into the retail space and showed him our work. He was impressed. Then he said it straight out. 'Zoey, I believe I am your father.' I was shocked, of course, after all this time. I had given up expecting him when I was a teenager. And for him to show up the week of my wedding."

Neither of the men said anything, so I felt I had to. "Honey, you're a huge success. There have been all kinds of stories about you in lifestyle magazines and sites on the internet. Anyone could have seen them, done a little research, and found the articles about your mother." I had done the same research, belatedly, the summer before, when Zoey was suspected of murder.

"I'm not a fool." Zoey's eyes blazed, and not only from the tears. "We agreed to do DNA tests. But he knew the stories! He knew about the conccrt. He knew about the paintings. He knew my mother's roommate's name. He was in prison, just like my mother told me he was."

She said this more triumphantly than is usually the case when announcing one's parent is incarcerated.

"Did he say where he was imprisoned, or what for?" Tom asked.

"Yes. Um. California. Fraud. He said it was a business deal that went wrong, the sale of a piece of art, and he was the fall guy."

I thought art fraud might get you a few years in prison, but not your child's entire thirty-seven-year lifetime. "Where has he been, did he say? Why didn't he find you sooner?"

"He knew Mom was murdered, and he had no idea where to find me. Then he saw an article about me on the Web. One of the ones you placed, Julia. Thank you. He kept searching and later found my wedding announcement. He thought that, with me getting married, and the possibility of children, it was time to finally connect."

"Why didn't you tell me?" Jamie struggled to keep the hurt from his voice, but I knew him so well I could hear it. Zoey could, too.

"It was so new. I've never had a father. I wanted to keep it to myself for a while." She paused. "Also, I didn't just believe everything he said. I wanted to wait for the DNA results to come back. Then I was going to tell you." She put her hand over Jamie's on the tabletop.

"You were going through so much by yourself." This time Jamie's voice didn't betray hurt, exactly. More like helplessness. And a realization that Zoey had been on her own for so long, the habits of her solitary life weren't completely gone. I was her best friend and her business partner. She hadn't told me, either.

"There was a painting my mother had done of my father," Zoey said. "It was in my room when I was little. Then it, too, was put away, and I never saw it again. I've tried to remember, to see if the figure was anything like the man who came to the studio. I couldn't tell. The painting was impressionistic, a blurry oil on canvas. My father was young in it, with dark hair. He carried more muscle on him. But all these years later, he would have changed. Could Kendall Clarkson have been my father? I wanted him to be. I have no blood relatives. I wanted him at my wedding. My only wedding." She smiled at Jamie. "This was my one chance."

"Did you actually take DNA tests?" Tom asked.

"No. We agreed we'd do that after I got back from my honeymoon."

"He planned to stay in town until you returned?" Tom sounded skeptical.

Zoey hesitated. "I think so. We didn't discuss it. He said he'd write away for the tests while I was gone, and we'd do them when I got back. I assumed that meant he'd stay. I didn't offer my apartment or anything. I was trying to be cautious, not to get carried away." The tears came again. "And now look what's happened."

"Did he say if he ever married or had a family?" Tom asked.

Zoey shook her head. "He said my mother was the love of his life."

CHAPTER SIXTEEN

Tom thanked Zoey "for being honest and brave." He gave his head a quick shake in the direction of the door. He wanted to go.

I looked at Jamie.

"I'm staying with Zoey." His tone discouraged argument.

"We weren't going to be together the night before our wedding." Zoey was still clinging to the idea that somehow, some way, she could salvage the wedding she had imagined.

"I'm staying," Jamie repeated.

"Of course," Tom said, and we left. Without talking about it, he and I slipped across the hall into the room I'd saved for him and sat on his bed. He wrapped me in his arms and held me tight.

"What now?" I asked from under his chin.

"You're going to bed," he answered. "You can sleep here. I'm going down to relieve Pete. It's late. It'll keep until morning. No one is leaving."

"Okay." He was right. We were exhausted and couldn't be bothering the guests any longer. I doubted I would sleep. Adrenaline was surging through my body, not least from Zoey's revelation about Kendall Clarkson's alleged identity. "I'll just go get my toothbrush and something to sleep in."

"I'll wait in the hall while you do. Then I'll walk you back, and you'll lock this door."

But as we crept along the hallway, Constance Marshall's door opened. "I heard Zoey crying."

"Jamie's with her," I assured her.

Constance ran her tongue around her lips as if they were dry, opened her mouth to speak, hesitated, and then opened her mouth again. "I have something more I need to tell you." She was looking at Tom, and I gathered that, whatever it was she had to say, it was in his official capacity.

"Of course," Tom said. "Let's not stand in the hall." He took my elbow as Constance backed up, and we made our way into her room.

We returned to our former positions, Tom on the desk chair, me on the bed, and Constance in the easy chair. The bed was still made. She'd evidently been sitting up since we'd left her, not trying to sleep.

She folded her hands in her lap.

"You had something to tell us." Tom spoke softly, as if coaxing a reluctant animal.

"Yes." Constance stopped, then began again. "You, really, but it's okay for Julia to be here. I wasn't fully honest with you before. I told you Kenneth Clark and I had lived together, long in the past. But I didn't tell you something important. When he left, he stole every penny I had." She stopped, searching both our faces. Tom's expression was one of sympathetic concern. I actually felt that way and hoped it showed.

"I was a young schoolteacher. I had a tiny savings account, enough money in checking for the next month's rent and groceries, and a ten-year-old car. Not much to take, but when he left, he took it all."

"He didn't own a gallery where he could show your paintings," I said.

"He did not. I'd known that for several months. He didn't have a job. He was always on the phone in my apartment. No cell phones in those days. He was wheeling and dealing, trying to buy and sell artwork. His big break was always just around the corner."

"What made you decide to tell me?" Tom asked.

"Two things, really." Constance tossed a long hank of gray hair back over her shoulder. "I want you to understand the character of the man whose murder you're investigating." She stopped, searching Tom's face to make sure her words had sunk in. "And I knew that, in the coming days, you would find out what happened, and it would make me look bad because I hadn't told you."

"How would I have found out?" Tom asked.

"I reported him to the police."

"I see." Tom's head pulled back as he raised his eyebrows. "Was he arrested? Was there a trial?"

Constance shook her head. "Neither. He was never found, as far as I know. My car was. It was returned to me months later. It had been abandoned on the other side of LA, where it was stripped. By then I had a new one."

"What did you do," I asked, "when this happened to you?"

"I was too embarrassed to tell anyone. My girlfriends, my parents. I told my dad my car had been stolen, and he loaned me money for a down payment on another one. I was able to pay my rent, though it was late. It was late for months, but my landlord was good to me, and eventually I caught up and got back on my feet."

"Is that why you and Clarkson were having heated words at the cocktail party?" I asked.

"Yes. I recognized him instantly. A rage I thought had left me long ago bubbled up inside. And then when he claimed he didn't know who I was! This person who had changed my life forever, made me fearful, caused me not to trust men until it was too late to have a family or a life of companionship. And it was all so little to him that he didn't remember me!"

"Did you kill him?" Tom asked it almost casually, but my breath caught in my throat. It had never occurred to me that Constance would have called us in to confess.

"No. I would have liked to kill him in that moment. I suppose I might have stabbed him with a toothpick from the shrimp cocktail, but I had no other weapon handy. I didn't know he'd be here."

"Have you talked to Zoey about this?" I asked.

"Never. Why should I talk to her about something that happened before she was born? It would have been a most unprofessional thing to tell a student. And even after our relationship extended into her adulthood, Zoey always looked to me for stability, for the small bit of mothering she got. I wouldn't have told her about my biggest mistake. It's not something I'm proud of." Constance rubbed her hands together, then looked at the window at the black night sky. "When I saw him here tonight, I had no idea who he was to Zoey. I wasn't going to ruin her beautiful party. And then, the next thing I knew, he was on the floor, gasping for air. And then you told me he was murdered."

When we left Constance, Tom thanked her and told her she should try to sleep. As she saw us to the door, she still looked exhausted, but somehow lighter. I thought she might at last be able to take his advice.

Back out in the hallway, Tom leaned against the wall. I thought it might be the only thing holding him up. My knees were rubbery, and everything I saw in the dim hall light was blurry, like I was swimming in a fishbowl.

"What does it all mean?" I asked.

"Our victim is a very, very bad guy who did very, very bad stuff to a lot of people. It caught up to him here on this little island."

"At his daughter's wedding."

"We don't know she's his daughter." Tom motioned toward my apartment door. "I'll wait for you while you get your stuff."

I didn't protest.

My living room was dark, but a light shone from the bathroom around the corner at the far end. I crept down there and entered the little passage between the bathroom and the bedroom. With the light on in the bathroom, I could see Zoey on her side on the bed, still in the bride pajamas. Jamie was behind her fully dressed, his arm protectively over her midsection.

I'd started to back up as quietly as I could when

Jamie sprang up off the bed, as if poked by a prod. "What?" he demanded. Seeing it was me, he advanced into the hall. "What's happened?"

"I'm so sorry," I whispered, backing into the living room. "I didn't mean to wake you. I'm just getting my stuff."

"I'm glad you came. You stay here." He was slipping into his shoes, which had been left in the living room.

"No, you stay. I'm going to sleep in Tom's room. He's gone downstairs to send Pete and Sonny to bed."

"No," Jamie insisted. "I want Zoey to wake up in the morning with you. I want some part of her wedding day to be as she imagined it."

That stopped me in my tracks. "Jamie, I'm not sure there can be a—"

He put a hand up to stop me. "I know, I know, I know. But I'm not going to give up on it until someone tells me I have to. The storm has stopped." He gestured to the windows on the other side of the room. The night was silent except for the creak of tree branches and the steady drip of water falling from the leaves. "That's obstacle one. We'll see what the morning brings on the other."

"I understand." I felt so bad for the guy. "Tom's in the hall. Tell him I'm staying here."

Jamie strode across the room. "Lock the door behind me."

I did. I put as much spin on it as I could so I was sure Tom could hear it turn on the other side. I went to the L. L. Bean tote on the far window seat that held my maid of honor pajamas. They were blue but otherwise matched Zoey's except for the exuberant label. Let her wake up in the morning seeing what she had wanted to see. I brushed my teeth and ran my hands through my hair. Eloise, the unsuspecting hairdresser, was at this moment sleeping in Busman's Harbor, thinking she was booked all morning to do the hair and makeup of the bride and her attendants. With a sigh that almost turned into a groan, I went to the bed and climbed into the spot that was still warm from Jamie's body. I put my arm around Zoey's middle, right where Jamie's had been.

"What's happened?" Zoey asked in her normal tone of voice.

I threw off my arm and turned on my back, bouncing us both on the mattress. "You're awake! You almost gave me a heart attack. Have you slept at all?"

"Not a wink, but I figured if I faked it, maybe Jamie could get some sleep. You didn't answer my question."

I told her Constance Marshall's story. It felt like a violation of Constance's privacy, but everything would be known in the morning. I thought Zoey had a right to know, if anyone did.

"He is my father." Zoey was sitting up, her back against the headboard.

I was cross-legged at the bottom of the bed. "Not proven. I believe Constance that Clarkson or Clark was her lover and stole her stuff, but that doesn't make him your father."

"But it does, don't you see? My mother had a type, and he was it. Horrible men who stole from her."

"Did your father steal from your mom? I thought she didn't have any money."

"Constance didn't either, from what you say. My

mother gave him an apartment to stay in. I assume they got food somehow. Not bad if you're hiding from the police."

"I'm not sure the dates match up."

"If he wasn't hiding because of Constance's complaint, it was something else. He was in prison by the time I was born. He is definitely my father."

Her eyes were bright and shining, her body tensed. I reached across and took her hand. I couldn't imagine she would sleep tonight, which meant, like a good friend, neither would I.

CHAPTER SEVENTEEN

But I did sleep. The exhaustion enveloped me, and I fell asleep lying across the bottom of the bed. Zoey slept, too, and we opened our eyes at the same time, startled into wakefulness by a sound outside.

The day was beautiful, the sun shining through scattered, high clouds. The trees and grass on the great lawn glowed with vibrant greens. The remaining damp would be burned off by the time the guests arrived. If the guests were allowed to come. If Zoey wanted to go on with it.

She trailed me into the main room of the apartment, and we stood for a moment, looking out at the navy-blue ocean, flat as a dinner plate. The perfect day for a wedding. The Whaler was tied up at the dock, looking as seaworthy as ever.

"What time is it?" Zoey rubbed an eye with her wrist.

I went back to the bedroom and retrieved my phone. "A little after eight," I called back to her.

"Oh, man. We've got to get going."

I was already pulling a Snowden Family Clambake sweatshirt over my pajama top. "Let me go find Tom and see what's going on."

I was answered by the sound of Zoey throwing up in the bathroom.

"Are you okay?" I didn't really want to get any closer but was ready to make the sacrifice if she needed me.

"I'm always fine right after I puke."

Thank goodness for small mercies. "Do you want me to send Jamie to you?"

"I can't see him before the wedding!"

Thinking that might mean she wouldn't see Jamie for some number of days or months, I left without comment.

Tom was on the front porch on his cell phone. "Service came back a few minutes ago," he mouthed at me, listening, and nodding as he did.

The call ended. "The medical examiner is on his way to meet the marine patrol to pick up our corpse. Lieutenant Binder will come out with them and a team."

"Good." I loved Tom, but he'd been up all night. I was glad his boss's steady hand would be on the tiller. "Just tell me this, are we having a wedding here in six hours?"

"The lieutenant hopes that we are. The crime scene is already destroyed. We moved the body twice. Whatever secrets it holds only the medical examiner can uncover. And the rain and wind have undoubtedly wiped out the rest of the evidence. The lieutenant is weighing the loss of a small, already-contaminated crime scene against the loss of fifty witnesses, who will presumably be here today and spread across the entire country by tomorrow. As soon as the techs get here, they'll search the dining pavilion and the area around it, but that won't take long. They'll be done by the time the guests arrive."

"Hmm . . . okay." This was unexpected news, and my brain flipped from wondering how I was going to tell Zoey the wedding was off to how I was going to tell her it was on. "Okay," I said again, shrugging. We'd been prepared to put on our first wedding in the renovated Windsholme yesterday, and we were, in all important ways, prepared to do it today. "If Zoey and Jamie agree."

"Of course. Can we talk to them now?"

"Zoey doesn't want to see Jamie before the wedding, so if we think this might happen, we'll have to talk to them separately."

"Jamie first," Tom said.

"Did you get any sleep?" I asked as we headed to the dining room.

"In the chair." He put a hand to his neck and moved it from one side to the other, the bones cracking so loudly I could hear them.

"I'm sorry."

"All part of the wedding-slash-homicide investigation service."

I gave him a grim laugh. Poor guy, he deserved at least my appreciation for his jokes.

Pete, Dan, and Jamie were all in the dining room, eating a hearty breakfast made by Livvie. Sonny, Jack, and Page were there, too. Page was bent over the phone she'd been deprived of since the previous evening, no doubt catching up with her friends. Constance and Bill arrived right behind Tom and me. They cast curious glances at Tom but went to the sideboard, which held chafing dishes filled with eggs and bacon, pancakes, and sausage, and plates of fruit and pastries. There was no sign of Derek or Amelia.

Jordan came in, smartly dressed in a clean white shirt and black pants and carrying a carafe of strong-smelling coffee.

I slowly became aware that everyone in the room, except Page, was looking at Tom. Finally, Dan Dawes broke the silence, "Are we having a wedding today or not?"

"That depends," Tom said. "Before I can answer, I need to borrow the groom. I'll be back soon to answer all your questions."

I sincerely doubted he'd answer *all* their questions.

I followed Jamie and Tom into the foyer. "I bet we are the least hungover groomsmen ever," I heard Pete saying to Dan as we left.

Well, there is that.

"Do you want to get married today?" Tom asked Jamie without preamble.

Jamie rubbed his hand across his chin. He hadn't shaved, and it made a rasping sound. "What does Zoey say?"

"I haven't asked her yet," Tom answered. "The first thing she'll ask me is what you want, so I thought I'd have that information in hand before we talk to her."

Jamie looked past Tom and me, gazing around the room where the ceremony would take place. Finally, he spoke. "My whole family is here. My parents and my aunts and uncles are in their eighties. I don't know how much longer they're going to be able to make the trip. If we do it later, I'm sure we'll do something small, and that's not what Zoey wants. And she wants to be married before the baby comes."

It was the first time Jamie had mentioned the baby. In the craziness and confusion of the previous night, I hadn't had a chance to tell Tom. I watched the emotions play across his face—surprise, then recovery, then, "Congratulations, Jamie. That's great. I'm happy for you both."

Jamie smiled, pleased, and maybe a little relieved to have the news out there.

"It could be her dad that died," I said. "Zoey may not be up for it."

"*Could be* her dad," Tom emphasized.

Jamie cleared his throat. "Whoever he was to her, a man was murdered. It's Zoey's decision. Tell her I'm up for it, but absolutely no pressure."

"Of course, I do!" Zoey answered Tom. "It's my wedding day. Can you think of a better day to get married?"

"Zoey, you don't have to," I assured her. "Say the word, and I will wind this whole thing down."

She looked at me, chin set. "Tom said we can have the wedding. We're having it."

My mind ticked through the million things that I had to do, that we all had to do. And the small amount of time we had to accomplish it.

Back down in the dining room, Tom made the announcement to cheers and applause. "The wedding is on."

Then it seemed like everyone was running everywhere all at once, off to get showered and dressed. The life seemed to have returned to the party.

But these people had had all night to get used to the idea that there was a dead man in the billiards room. I didn't think we could keep the information from spreading among the other guests when they arrived. I hoped the news, sanitized as it would be with the man's body off the island and the event firmly in the past, however recent, wouldn't put a damper on the wedding.

At that moment, Derek and Amelia arrived in the dining room. Like Tom, they were dressed in the same clothes they'd had on the day before. They didn't have anything else.

"When's breakfast?" Amelia chirped.

"Coffee's still up," I said, indicating the carafe on the sideboard. "I'll see what I can find in the kitchen."

"Who takes us back to our B and B to get changed?" Derek asked me.

I looked at Tom. Sonny had already left to get the florist, caterer, hairdresser, and photographer.

"I'd prefer you remain here," Tom said.

"I can't go to a wedding like this!" Amelia's clambake outfit was cute, but casual.

Particularly not the wedding of your boyfriend's ex.

"Tell you what," Tom said, with every appearance of reasonableness. "I have colleagues coming over from the mainland soon. Tell me the name of your accommodation, and they'll bring your stuff over. You can get changed here."

"No!" Amelia and Derek reacted in unison.

"No way," Derek added. "You can't force us to stay here. I know my rights."

"No way are your cops going through my underwear." Amelia was indignant. I wouldn't have appreciated it either.

"We have a female detective coming—" Tom started.

"Or going through our stuff, period." Derek talked over him, red in the face.

"Where are you staying?" I asked.

Amelia lifted her shoulders, "I have no idea what it's called."

But Derek answered, "The Snuggles Inn."

"I know the owners well. They'll be here at the wedding later. What if I call over there and ask one of them to retrieve the things from your room? No police need enter, and they can give everything to the detectives to bring to you. Otherwise, you'll have to wait until the rest of the guests arrive, when the Snugg sisters can bring your stuff."

Derek looked undecided, but Amelia jumped on the offer. I called the Snuggles Inn and got Vee, much the better sister to handle requests for a cosmetic kit and complicated underwear.

I handed the phone to Amelia and went to the kitchen to get them some breakfast while she talked to Vee.

While Derek and Amelia ate, I cleared the dirty dishes off the table, intending to help Livvie clean up before the catering crew arrived. From the kitchen window, I saw several boats tie up at our dock. Tom huddled with Lieutenant Binder and a group of official-looking people. Then Tom walked them to the dining pavilion, pointing out where the man had fallen off the bench and where we'd taken him behind the gift-shop counter. A crime-scene tech took photographs, and several uniformed state troopers fanned out, searching the lawn. Tom, Binder, and the medical examiner approached Windsholme.

By the time the kitchen was clean, Sonny arrived with our Boston Whaler. I spotted the catering crew and their load of still more plastic containers and cardboard boxes. They were bringing over all the food that wasn't already here, except for the elaborate five-tiered wedding cake. Another one of Zoey's bows to tradition, it was coming later with the guests on the much more stable *Jacquie II*. The tall woman who must be Jordan's mother was with the caterers, looking competent and strong as she helped load Cassie Howard's arms with containers and then picked up more with her own.

Eloise, the hairdresser-slash-makeup artist, disembarked along with her several cases and pieces of equipment. The photographer came with her camera cases and lights. The florist was the last one off. She and Sonny reached back into the boat and retrieved the boxes containing the centerpieces for every table, the bouquets for Zoey, Livvie and me, and the boutonnieres for the men. A huge box must hold the floral swag, as long as the grand staircase, and another the flowered arch under which Jamie and Zoey would be married. The flowers were a riot of blues, pinks, and lavenders, the colors of the wedding. I smiled automatically when I saw them, excited about the wedding for the first time. Thoughts of logistics and murder investigations disappeared momentarily. All the challenges of the day would return, but it was a moment of pure joy, and I savored it.

"You go first," I said to Livvie, pointing to the hairdresser. Two uniformed state troopers escorted the group up toward the house, keeping them at the edge of the great lawn, far away from the dining pavilion. "I may be needed by the detectives."

"Needed?" Livvie teased. "*You* may need to find out what's going on. That's not the same thing." Nonetheless, she agreed to my plan. "I'll get the caterers settled. My dress is at the little house. I'll retrieve it and report for a blow-dry and an updo."

"Thanks." I hugged my sister. "You're the best."

CHAPTER EIGHTEEN

I found Tom and Binder at a table in the main salon, deep in conversation. From what I overheard as I came closer, Tom was finishing up briefing Lieutenant Binder on everything that had happened during the night.

"Was it murder?" I asked before they could speak.

"It wasn't an allergic reaction," Binder answered. "Tom's instincts were correct there. And the victim definitely took a needle to the back of his ear. Good catch by Dawes. Beyond that, the medical examiner can't say until he's back in his facility. So we're treating the death as suspicious and your dining pavilion as a crime scene."

As he talked, I looked out the window and watched Livvie attempt to get her dress from the little house. A state trooper stopped her and urged her back in the direction of Windsholme. Livvie argued, gesticulating and pointing. Finally, worn down, he escorted her across the lawn to get her dress.

"Why are we going ahead with this wedding?" I

asked. "And more important, how do I know the guests and my staff and contractors are safe?"

"I'll be here," Binder said calmly. "Check out my suit."

I'd registered something was different about his appearance, but it wasn't until he pointed it out that I noticed that his usual sports jacket had been dispensed with and he was wearing a rather handsome and well-fitting charcoal suit.

I nodded my approval, and Binder went on. "I brought Tom's suit. Four more detectives will be here, appropriately dressed. There will be half a dozen Busman's Harbor police here, too, already invited as guests of Jamie's. They'll be briefed. I'm going to talk to Jamie and Pete after this." Binder caught the look on my face. "Don't worry. We clean up nicely."

I tried for a more neutral expression. Did I want this wedding to go on? The answer was yes, because Zoey and Jamie did. What was I going to do with five extra police detectives?

Not the time to be thinking about the seating chart, Julia.

"There is an advantage to having cell service and the internet," Binder said. "And access to databases. Fingerprints will confirm his identity, but we know a whole lot about Kenneth Clark aka Kendall Clarkson."

Tom looked like he was sitting upright due to willpower alone. I wondered if Binder noticed. Would I be able to persuade Tom to take a nap, or at least a shower, before the wedding? It was unlikely duty would allow for it.

"Clarkson's well known by California and federal authorities," Binder was saying. "Mostly white-collar crimes. Selling the same piece of artwork a dozen or so times, and then not paying the owner once. That sort of thing. He's been a guest in both California state and federal prisons a dozen times."

Tom nodded. "I told you we had a similar story here involving two guests—selling the artwork and not paying the artist and his agent. Were there also complaints from women that he'd robbed them or conned them out of money?"

"No," Binder said, "but from what you told me, the complaint from Constance Marshall was to local LAPD forty years ago, and Clarkson was never charged or tried. Nothing I've found goes back that far."

"Zoey thinks Clarkson may have done the same thing to her mom," I told them. "Left and took what little she had."

"If that's the case," Tom said, "he doesn't seem to care about the money particularly. He doesn't target rich women. At least he didn't back then."

"More like vulnerable women," I said.

"Vulnerable women who are artists or at least connected to the art world in some way," Tom added.

"Was he in prison when Zoey was born?" I asked.

"First thing I confirmed," Binder said. "Five-year stretch started two months before Zoey was born. He served the full sentence."

That fit with Zoey's mom's story. I wondered, which was worse? To have a con man pretend to be the father you would never meet, or to meet your father, spend one, uncertain hour with him, and then have him murdered? I would personally have been happier with the status quo. Zoey hadn't expected her father at her wedding and would have been fine if he hadn't come. But I couldn't pretend to know what Zoey would have chosen.

"Will you do a DNA test if the fingerprints are inconclusive?" I asked.

"The fingerprints should be pretty good," Binder said. "You both properly noticed the absence of swelling of the corpse. But we will do DNA. We have samples from Clarkson in the system to compare. It will take longer but will also be more conclusive."

"Is there a way Zoey can get the DNA results? Can you take her DNA and compare it? Or get her a sample of his DNA to submit for testing on her own?"

I didn't miss Tom's doubtful expression, but Binder was more encouraging. "It will take a lot of time, and paperwork, and maybe a judge's order, but since she may have been his nearest relative, perhaps it can be done. I'll see what I can do."

Through the window, I saw one of the crime-scene techs straighten up and shout something to the trooper standing across from him. The trooper came toward Windsholme at a jog. We got to the front porch in time to hear him call, "Lieutenant, sergeant, we've found something!"

I wasn't allowed to get close. Binder and Tom squinted at a small object on the very edge of the lawn where it turned to woods. There was a lot of standing around and measuring distances. While I watched, I was relieved to see the medical examiner and marine-patrol officers roll a gurney down the lawn toward the dock with a black body bag on it. The medical examiner stopped and conferred with Lieutenant Binder, then looked at whatever it was they had found.

I was aware of the tick-tick-tick of the clock. I had to get on with it.

I went to help the florist, who was stringing the elaborate garland down the grand staircase. I was up on a ladder when I heard footsteps behind me. "Can you come down for a minute?" Tom steadied the ladder. Binder stood at his shoulder.

"Just let me get this"—I grunted with the effort—"wire around the banister." The florist had gone to fetch the swag for the arch. Taking advantage of her absence and a momentary lull in the busy foyer, I asked, "What did you find? The needle?"

"Not yet," Tom answered. "It was an empty refill bottle for e-cigarettes. There would have been enough nicotine in there to kill a person."

My eyes widened as I took this in. "You can buy enough poison in a smoke shop to kill someone?"

"So the ME tells us." Binder said. "Personally, I've never seen a case of purposeful nicotine poisoning before. And we may not have seen one now. The medical examiner will let us know."

"How long will that take?" I asked.

Binder shrugged. "Days, probably. If he'd ingested something containing nicotine, there might be a chance the pathologist could smell it in the stomach contents. But since we think it was injected, the only indication will be in the body chemistry."

I thought for a moment. "Dan Dawes told us he was out on the back porch having a smoke during the storm. Might he have thrown the empty bottle

into the woods? Did you notice a package of cigarettes in his room?" I asked Tom.

"No," he answered, "but I didn't see any vaping
apparatus, either."

"Wait a minute." Lieutenant Binder pulled his
phone back out and went scrolling through his
notes. "Did you say Dan Dawes?"

"That's right, Daniel Dawes," Tom answered.
"He was the one who was sitting next to Clarkson
when he keeled over."

Binder was still scrolling. "I didn't catch the
name before, or I wasn't following. But I do recognize it. Daniel Dawes—lives in Los Angeles, right?
There's a complaint from him against Clarkson
from ten years ago. He said he paid a hundred and
fifty thousand dollars for some arty pottery that
was never delivered."

It can't be, I thought, as I followed the men up
the stairs. Not possible. Could Dan Dawes be the
person who'd bought Bill Lascelle's artwork and
been swindled by Kendall Clarkson? It seemed so
improbable, yet this case seemed to swirl in on itself like a whirlpool.

Dan Dawes lived in Los Angeles.

Dan Dawes was rich.

When asked if he collected art, Dan had said he
"dabbled."

The groomsmen were in Jamie's room, fully
dressed in their tuxedos, with the boutonnieres in
their lapels. The three of them looked so handsome. The tuxedo even smoothed out Pete's
rounder figure.

"Julia!" Jamie frowned when he saw me. "Why aren't you dressed?"

"I'm on my way there," I reassured him. "Just this one stop."

"Mr. Dawes, I'm Lieutenant Binder, Maine State Police Major Crimes Unit." Binder stuck out a hand.

"I gathered," Dan said, shaking it.

"We'd like to ask you a few questions. Maybe we could go to your room here. It won't take long."

Dan looked at Jamie, who smiled. "Sure."

Dan's bedroom was as neat as a pin, no clothes littered about, no shaving things on the vanity in the bathroom. He was packed and ready to leave the island when the *Jacquie II* sailed tonight.

We huddled together in the center of the room. Binder had promised to be quick. They hadn't asked me to come along, but they hadn't told me to go away, either.

"I understand that you're a smoker," Binder began. "What brand do you smoke?"

I was interested that Binder didn't ask the direct question—cigarettes or e-cigarettes.

"American Spirits." Dan answered without hesitation.

"Can you show me your pack?" Binder sounded casual, like he might try to bum a smoke.

Dan raised an eyebrow in inquiry but played along. "Sure."

I could have sworn there was nothing in his inside pockets, the tuxedo jacket fell so nicely on him. But he pulled out a dark yellow package of cigarettes, only slightly crumbled.

"Thank you," Tom said. "You can put them away."

"You were sitting next to Mr. Clarkson when his attack began, is that correct?" Binder asked.

Dan nodded.

"And you had never met Mr. Clarkson before?" Binder put the question deliberately, not like he was confirming the information. More like he was giving Dan a chance to change his story.

Dan was a smart man, a man who noticed subtleties. He swallowed, and a series of emotions crossed his face in quick succession—doubt, fear, and then resolution. He shrugged inside the jacket, squaring his shoulders, and looked directly at the lieutenant. "I suspect you wouldn't be asking that if you didn't know something different."

Binder nodded. "Why don't you tell me about it."

"I assume you've discovered that I had an unpleasant interaction with Mr. Clarkson ten years ago." Binder nodded, and Dan went on. "I was stupid. I had money in my pocket for the first time in my life and a big, sterile office space I wanted to look a little classier, a little warmer. I had always been interested in ceramics and glass, but I never had money to spend on it. A decorator took me to a preview for Lascelle's show. I bought every piece on the spot. Except, I didn't, as it turned out."

"What happened?" Tom asked.

"I suspect you know what happened if you have the complaint. I gave Clarkson the money, a cashier's check. I later learned you're supposed to present the check on delivery of the art. Live and learn. Clarkson never delivered. He disappeared. Look, you can't think that I killed him for it. It was ten years ago, and I've more than recovered from the loss. I'm sorry I didn't tell you." He looked at

Tom and me. "But it meant nothing to me. All I ever wanted was to forget about it."

"Yet you reported it to the police at the time," Binder said.

"I had to for insurance purposes. I knew I'd never see the money or the artwork again. As it turned out, the insurance didn't pay out, either. I had no proof I'd ever owned the ceramics."

"Nonetheless, it must have been a shock to see Clarkson here," Tom said.

"It wasn't. He'd aged. His hair had gone white, and I'd never seen him with the mustache. I only met with him face-to-face twice. I wasn't sure it was him until he sat down beside me and introduced himself."

"What did you say?" I asked, fascinated.

"At first, I ignored him. I was having a nice night with my grandparents, whom I hardly ever get to see. It was my uncle's wedding rehearsal. I wanted it to be fun."

Something in his voice made me say, "And then?"

"And then, he started bragging to my dad about what a big deal he was, how he owned this gallery in LA, showed famous artists. I sat there with my blood boiling. Finally, I turned to him and demanded, 'Do you know who I am?' At that very moment, he turned red, gasped, and fell off the bench. You guys ran over. I thought you were going to Heimlich him, but instead Pete started banging on his chest and then you dragged him behind the counter. End scene. Can I go now?"

"Just a moment," Tom said. "You were right next to him when it happened. Did you see anything, anything at all that might have precipitated the event?"

Dan shook his head. "Nothing. As I've said, the waiter delivered his Manhattan. Clarkson said, 'Thank you, Jordan.' I asked for a gin and tonic. The waiter moved off. Clarkson was on the ground. The end."

"He called the waiter by his name?" Tom was surprised. "You didn't mention that before."

"Didn't I?" Dan replied. "I thought I did."

CHAPTER NINETEEN

"It doesn't mean anything." I trailed Binder and Tom down the hallway. "We tell our wait-staff to introduce themselves to each table. That way the diners can hail them by name if they need them. Also, it improves the tips."

"Clarkson wasn't with the group when they sat down," Tom argued. "He wouldn't have heard the introduction."

"Jordan told him later." We were on the landing at the top of the stairs by that point. I lowered my voice because an army of people was running back and forth below, readying the foyer for the ceremony and preparing the main salon for the meal.

"We have to talk to the kid, Julia," Binder whispered. "You know that. Our victim fell over right after Jordan left him."

"Fine." I put my foot down. I didn't stomp, but apparently unconsciously I picked it up and put it down again, causing both Tom and I to stare at my sneaker-shod foot in surprise. "Fine." I sounded short, but I was serious. "But could you please talk to him after the dinner? This is an island. He's not going anywhere. And you," I turned to Tom, "need to get dressed. And so do I."

Binder hesitated, but then gave in. "Okay. Okay."

"Good. I'm going to—shoot!"

Down at the dock, a marine patrol boat had arrived with Binder's additional detectives, all four dressed for a wedding, as Binder had promised. The lone woman, wearing a stylish blue suit, held a bright green cocktail dress on a hanger.

I ran to the dock to collect Derek and Amelia's stuff to deliver it to their room. They would no doubt have a few choice words to say about the late timing.

But when I got to their door, laden with hanging dress, garment bag, makeup kit, and a canvas bag that I suspected contained underwear, Derek wasn't there.

"Come in." Amelia sniffled from behind the door when I knocked. "It's open."

"Where's Derek?" I hung her dress and his suit on the closet door.

"Dunno. Don't care."

I had told Tom and Binder and the other detectives that they couldn't deliver the clothes. I knew what would happen if any of them got into that room, and there wasn't time for questioning witnesses. That was why I was schlepping all the stuff on my own. Mercifully, Tom had gone to shower, and Binder was bringing the rest of the team up to speed.

But here was Amelia, alone, sitting on an unmade bed, crying. I couldn't leave her like that. I sat next to her, but didn't touch her. "What's the matter?"

"What isn't?" That brought a fresh round of crying. Fortunately, I'd supplied the room with a box of tissues. I fetched it and handed one to her.

Eventually, she stopped crying enough to talk. "I agreed to come with Derek on this trip for several reasons. For one, there was no way he wasn't going to come to Zoey's wedding, and I didn't want him to come alone. Not that I thought he was going to stand up and object at the ceremony or anything. I only wanted him to remember I'm alive. But the main reason was curiosity. I was dying to meet this paragon of womanhood—talented, beautiful, successful, everything that I'm not."

"You've met her now. What do you think?" I asked.

"I wanted to dislike her. I hated her before I met her. But she's been lovely to me, even when I've been terrible to her. She talked to me like I was a regular, interesting person. She wanted to know about my art. It's her wedding weekend. I would have understood if she was distracted. But she was kind."

"Zoey is kind."

"I hoped before we came that Derek would see her as she is today, older, and in love with someone else. Then he might realize he was holding on to someone who didn't exist anymore." Amelia hunched in on herself, looked at the floor, but then looked up at me. "But that isn't how it worked out. Just the opposite. I think Derek fell in love again. You saw him." She turned to me. "He's like a puppy dog around her. All bright eyes and wagging his tail. It's disgusting."

"And disrespectful," I added, "to you."

"And disrespectful," she agreed. "Everyone here saw it. Zoey was lovely and patient with him. She never told him to go away, but she steered him back to me whenever she could."

"She probably sensed your discomfort," I said.

"My discomfort was there for everyone to see."

"But that's not all." Something more was troubling her.

"That's not even the half of it." Tears squeezed from the corners of her eyes. "Do you see what she looks like?"

"She looks like you." Making Amelia the most reboundy of rebound girlfriends. The shadow twin.

It must be so hurtful. I hadn't liked her. She'd been brittle and demanding, even allowing for the tough spot she was in. But I couldn't help but feel for her. What was she—twenty-two, twenty-three?

"She looks like me because I'm her sister." And then Amelia broke down completely.

Which was a good thing because I couldn't speak. I felt like I'd taken a punch to the gut. How many relatives was Zoey going to have crawling out of the woodwork this weekend?

"Why do you think she's your sister?" Amelia had calmed down and was hiccupping into a tissue. It had to be more than the resemblance. But then my mind began to tick off other things. Their Los Angeles origins. That Amelia had said she was an artist, like Zoey.

"I think she's my sister because *he* was here. My father. Her father, too. He must be. Why else would he have been at her rehearsal dinner?"

My brain disappeared for a moment. I couldn't process the information. Finally, I asked. "Mr. Clark-

son? The man who was murdered was your father?"
I flashed on the scene at the cocktail party when
Amelia had very deliberately turned her back on
the man in the blue blazer and then crowded in,
protecting Zoey.

"Do you know the expression 'things can't get
any worse'?" Amelia asked.

I smiled despite the tension in the room. "It's
usually said right before—or, more often, right
after—things have gotten much worse."

Amelia nodded. "Exactly." Now that she'd decided to tell me, she seemed to find momentum.
"I thought coming here with Derek would result in
a horrible week. Then it got so much worse." She
blew her nose. "I never knew my dad. I was raised
by my grandparents. My mother was . . ." Amelia
made a motion with her hand that might mean
anything from "took off," to "crazy," to "in an iron
lung." I didn't probe.

"My grandparents didn't know who my father
was. When I became an adult, I started looking. I
spit in a test tube and sent the spit off. I didn't
think about it much after that. I'd taken a big step
and was content to wait. Maybe he was looking,
too. Maybe he wasn't. I was fine either way. Or I
told myself I was."

I made a sympathetic sound, and she went on.
"Then this man showed up at my work. He was
handsome, dressed in nice clothes. Very respect-
able. He asked if I was Lauren Gerhart's daughter.
One bit of conversation led to another. He said he
was my dad. We went to a café and talked for
hours. He knew everything about my mom. Not
just what she looked like, but what she'd studied in

college, what her favorite song was. Her favorite
color—even I didn't know that. He told me things
about my grandparents that I didn't know, and I
lived with them for eighteen years."

"Where did he say he'd been all those years?"

"He said he hadn't known about me. That he'd
run into my mom recently, at a music festival. That
tracked. And she'd told him. That's how he knew
how to find me, which surprised me, because I didn't
think Mom knew where I was.

"I wasn't a fool." She thrust her chin at me, as if
daring me to say she was. They were the exact words
Zoey had used. "I had him take a DNA test with
the same company I'd used. I thought it would
come back he was my father. But the tests take
time. We had to order the kit, have him spit in the
tube, and send it back. All during the wait, I was
spending time with Ken." Her eyes started to well.
"He told me to call him dad." She stopped, drawing in her breath in great gulps. I was afraid she
wouldn't be able to go on, but she squared her
shoulders and continued.

"He said it was too expensive for him to stay in
his hotel while we waited for the results. I invited
him to stay at my place. He was there for two
months." She stopped, bright red with embarrass-
ment.

I knew where this was going. "Then left with any
money you had and anything else of value." I said
it because I thought it would be hard for her to say.

She didn't seem surprised that I'd guessed. "Yes.
My car, every bit of cash I had, including in my
checking and savings, and a pearl necklace from
my grandmother."

I wasn't sure she would welcome it, but I put my hand on her shoulder. "I'm sorry. That must have been terrible."

"Terrible emotionally and financially." The tears that had been threatening spilled over again. "I had no money. The amount he stole was trivial, but it set me back for months."

"I'm sorry," I said again and waited while she dabbed her eyes. "What about the DNA?"

"I watched him spit into the tube. I mailed the sample myself. I waited for weeks and weeks. I wanted to know even more after he was gone. But the company claimed they never received it. I couldn't understand it for the longest time, but then I realized that he must have removed the label before he put it in the envelope, so they couldn't match the sample to his registration. That's the only thing that makes sense."

"How long ago was this?"

"Three and a half years."

What Clarkson had done to Constance Marshall was awful enough, but doing something even crueler to this fatherless girl turned my stomach. "Don't you think the fact that he sabotaged the DNA test means he's not your dad?" And therefore, not Zoey's dad. "Plus, he stole from you. Wouldn't that mean you aren't his kid?"

That got me a raised eyebrow from Amelia. "You've never had a parent steal from you? You must have great parents."

I did have two wonderful parents. My dad had died when I was twenty-five, and I missed him terribly, but he'd left the best of himself for me to treasure.

"Either he's not my dad and it was all a con," she

said quietly, "or he is, and I won the genetic lottery, two awful parents."

"At the party, you avoided him because you didn't want to confront him," I said.

"I spotted him on the boat and almost fell overboard. How in the world did Zoey or Jamie know him? But then I saw Zoey. My heart beat faster. I began to sweat and was tongue-tied. Not the way you want to meet your boyfriend's ex. Suddenly, the stakes were huge. I wanted to know everything about her, and not just because she's Derek's ex."

"Did you tell anyone about your history with Kendall Clarkson?" I asked. "Did Derek know the story before you came here, even if he didn't know a name or a face?"

"I never told Derek. I never told anyone. Not before."

"Not even your grandparents?"

"They're the last people I would tell. What would be the point? I told you they never knew who my father was. It would only upset them."

"But you did tell Derek at some point this weekend?"

"About an hour ago."

I didn't like Derek, but I had to admit he wasn't stupid. He would have put it all together—Clarkson leaving Zoey's studio, embracing her, her tears, Clarkson showing up at the rehearsal dinner, apparently a surprise to everyone except Zoey. Clarkson had been running the same con on Zoey that he had on Amelia. What would Derek do with that knowledge?

Amelia exhaled noisily and stood. "I have to get dressed."

She still planned to go to the wedding. "You

don't have to. I can find you someplace in the house to stay. You don't have to see Derek."

She shook her head. "I want to see Zoey get married. She's my sister."

I had to get a move on, too. I started for the door and turned back. "Please, don't tell Zoey your big secret until after the reception. She'd be thrilled to have a sister, but she's already absorbed too many blows this weekend. Tell her after."

Amelia turned, holding her bright green dress up in front of her. "Okay," she said. "I understand."

CHAPTER TWENTY

I dashed back to my apartment, hoping no one would waylay me with a question. When I rushed through the door, I stopped dead.

Zoey stood in the center of my living room in her white dress. She turned when she heard me and smiled her big smile. She was so stunning I thought I might burst into noisy, sleep-deprived tears.

I'd seen the dress before, but only with sneakers poking out underneath it when she found it or with a tailor bobbing around with pins in her mouth at a fitting. Never like this. The dress was a marvel, the definition of traditional, the word Zoey had said over and over throughout the planning process. It was white, of course, and perfectly fitting, showing off her curves and, through some kind of designer magic, lengthening her short waist. It was the perfect match of bride and gown.

Eloise had tamed Zoey's curls and woven flowers in her hair. Makeup had somehow wiped away the near-sleepless night and the tears. The woman

I most often saw in a bandanna, with clay-spattered
hands and paint under her fingernails, looked like,
not a queen or a princess or a goddess, but like a
woman who owned the day, who loved her life and
couldn't wait for the future.

The photographer was snapping pictures, her
smile as big as the bride's.

"You look so beautiful!" I hugged her, careful of
her hair, the makeup, and the dress.

Livvie stood by the fireplace in a lavender gown
that showed off her broad shoulders and trim
waist. She was looking at Zoey and beaming like a
mother hen. It hit me then like a blow to the chest.
How much Zoey must be missing her mother.

Eloise, who had made Livvie and Zoey beautiful,
was glaring at me, her hairdryer clutched in her
hand like a gun. "You're late!"

"I'm sorry." I ran toward the bathroom. "I'm
going to shower."

"No time!" Eloise shouted.

"I'm a very fast showerer."

"That's a lie!" Livvie called after me, but then
she laughed.

I had to get the dirt of the long night off me.
Eloise and her suitcase full of makeup could only
do so much. I set a record for cleanliness and pre-
sented myself to her, my blond hair dripping. She
tut-tutted but swung into action. I closed my eyes
as she brushed and blew and for the first time
since I'd entered my apartment, thought about
what Amelia had told me. The sight of Zoey in her
gown had pushed every other thought from my
head. Whatever the truth of the matter, Zoey would
treat Amelia as she had all along, with kindness.

I hadn't treated Amelia with kindness. I hadn't

even really seen her or thought of her apart from Derek. She'd been Zoey's ex's plus-one. I'd put her in that box and left her there. Even after she'd made a point to say she too was an artist from Los Angeles. Even after I'd seen her deliberately turn her back on Kendall Clarkson at the cocktail party. Tom hadn't taken her seriously, either. It had to have been from tiredness. He was a better cop than that.

Eloise finished with my hair, which she'd pulled tight to my head and coiled in the back. I thought it suited me. The only thing was that, with no hair to frame it, my face looked even worse. I hoped she could work the same miracle with the dark circles and puffy eyes that she had with Zoey.

When I was done, Livvie and Zoey both exclaimed over the transformation. Even Eloise murmured that I looked all right. They helped me into my pale blue dress, maneuvering it around the hair and the makeup. The dress had been a bit of a debacle. Livvie and I might be sisters, but she looked like our dad, tall, broad-shouldered, with auburn hair and hazel eyes. I was petite and blond like our mom. It was ironic that Zoey and Amelia, who might not even be sisters, looked far more alike than Livvie and me. There was no way we were wearing the same dress. I'd gone for more coverage, a princess neckline, and a fitted waist. The same miracle worker who had altered Zoey's gown had fitted my dress, and it fell perfectly. I ran to my closet for my shoes and returned to model the full ensemble.

Eloise touched up my lipstick. The photographer took candid and posed shots of the three of us. "You all look wonderful," Eloise said. "I'll get my stuff later." I told her there was food in the kitchen. She'd have to wait for the *Jacquie II* to get home that night.

The photographer packed her equipment and left to prepare for the ceremony. The apartment was suddenly quiet.

Zoey poured champagne for Livvie and me and fizzy water for herself, and we toasted. "To your day," I said. "Your happy day."

Zoey smiled, not bravely or nervously, but with genuine, starry-eyed happiness. I began to believe that everything might be all right. She raised her glass. "I never had a family, and now I'm gaining Jamie's. He has two sisters and two sisters-in-law, but you two are the sisters of my heart. I will always love you."

The tears that welled in me were not from tiredness or nerves, but from love. Livvie put a knuckle to her eye. "Our makeup," she cried. And we all laughed, and hugged, ready to meet the day.

The ship's horn aboard the *Jacquie II* sounded, and the boat pulled up to the dock. "The guests are here!" We clinked again, and giggled and cried again, just like the bride and her attendants are supposed to.

CHAPTER TWENTY-ONE

I watched through the window across from the second-floor landing as the uniformed state troopers escorted the guests up the great lawn on the opposite side from the dining pavilion. It wasn't the usual route, and I was sure it caused commentary. Several people looked across toward the place where Kendall Clarkson had fallen off his picnic bench. The police had removed the crime-scene tape, but still . . .

Below us, Pete and Dan handed programs to guests as they entered the foyer and found places to stand. The noise of voices grew, welling up to where we stood on the landing above. With final good-luck hugs for Zoey, Livvie and I slipped down the back stairs from my mother's apartment into the kitchen.

Jamie, Pete, and Dan stood at the front of the foyer under the flowered swag. Livvie and I slid in through the swinging door and took our places opposite. Bill Lascelle played an old folk tune softly on his guitar. Despite whatever they may have seen or thought when they walked past the dining pavilion, the crowd was happy and chatty, full of anticipation.

The music changed, and everyone looked up. Conversation stopped immediately. Zoey started down the grand staircase in her beautiful white dress, just as she'd dreamed. All eyes were on her.

Jamie met her at the bottom of the stairs and escorted her to the front.

Constance began the ceremony. "Dearly beloved, we are gathered here . . ." She was a former teacher, and I was sure she could be heard in the back row.

The kitchen had quieted for the ceremony. The caterers and waitstaff stood respectfully on the outer perimeter of the oval-shaped room. I picked out Jordan and the woman who had to be his mother, Mel.

The photographer was discreet, as Zoey had instructed. The click of the camera was the only sign she was present.

My mother was in the first row of guests, holding hands with Captain George. Her smile was so wide I thought it must hurt. I could tell she was proud of her daughters, and I stood up even straighter. "My beautiful girls," she mouthed and then returned her attention to Zoey and Jamie. She was happy for them, especially for Jamie, the little boy she'd watched grow up. More than anything, she was happy herself for the first time in years.

There is something about a wedding that makes couples think of their own weddings and partnerships. Jamie's parents, married more than fifty years, let their tears fall freely, their arms entwined. Sonny, the old softy, stared at my sister with googly eyes. Even Gus suffered to let Mrs. Gus hold his arm and lean on him in public.

My eyes sought Tom, standing at the back of the room by the front door. He noticed me looking, grinned back, and mouthed, "I love you." I couldn't say it back without distracting from the bride and groom, so I smiled and sent the thought back silently.

Jamie and Zoey had written their own vows. I'd been skeptical, though I didn't say anything. Zoey was a visual person, a hands-on person. Anything to do with writing, even developing our product descriptions, was part of the job I had taken from her because she disliked it. Jamie was the same, a restless guy who wanted to be out of police headquarters, on the street. He regarded the paperwork as the worst part of the job.

But I'd been wrong. Each of them had taken the time to know what the other most needed to hear.

"James, I give you my life, for life," Zoey said. "We will make a home and be safe there in our love. When times are hard, we will prop each other up to give each other the strength to face them. When there is joy, we will multiply it, and spread it to all we love and all who love us." When she finished, she smiled at him, a little uncertainly, and nodded for him to speak.

"Zoey, my love." Jamie's voice was thick with emotion, "all my life, I've felt like a part of me was missing, until you came and filled the empty places, even those I didn't know were there. I give you my family, the one I was born to and the one we will create. I give you a home where you will always be safe. Whatever the future holds, I will be at your side, cheering you on, loving and supporting you. Your success is my success; your challenges are my challenges. We are one team, held together by respect and love, now and forever."

There wasn't a dry eye in the house when they finished. I worked hard to suppress my tears, but salty liquid backed up in my throat, and I watched in horror as a large drip exited my nose and landed on one of the two bouquets I held, mine and Zoey's. I looked around, checking to see if anyone had noticed, but all eyes were on the bride and groom, as if they were the only people in the room.

Constance led them through the exchange of rings. Pete played it straight, handing them over with appropriate solemnity. Zoey and Jamie promised to honor and cherish but not obey. Even tradition had its limits. And then he kissed her with an exuberance that nearly knocked a flower from her hair.

A great cheer went up and a round of applause. Jamie blushed appealingly, and Zoey laughed, a joyful sound that carried above the rest of the noise. The guitar started up, and everyone began to talk at once.

As people moved into the main salon, Tom came across the room as if propelled by a rocket and took me in his arms. "Success," he said. "Your first wedding in Windsholme, and it was beautiful."

"Thank you." I kissed him. "Thank you for everything you've done for me."

"I love you," he said, out loud this time.

"I love you, too." I said it out loud, too.

* * *

In the main salon, we formed a receiving line, another of Zoey's bows to tradition. "I want to see the face of every person at my wedding," she had said. "I want to thank them for coming and remember them forever." Jamie, Livvie, Pete, and I were in the room at the time, and not one of us was in a position to argue. None of us were married except Livvie, who'd had six people at her wedding, none of whom she was ever likely to forget.

"I'm sorry to hear that the cow died. I'm sorry to hear that the cow died. I'm sorry to hear that the cow died," Gus muttered as he came along the receiving line, shaking hands. I held on to his, not letting him go. "It's what I always say at these things," he grumped. "Proves no one ever listens. "

Perhaps he had a point. He'd made it past Pete, Dan, Constance, and Livvie without any of them noticing.

"And I say," Mrs. Gus was right behind Gus, "so lovely to see you. What a wonderful ceremony. Isn't the bride beautiful?" She looked pointedly at her husband. "There, that was easy." She looked back at me. "You look beautiful, too." She kissed me on the cheek.

After they passed through the receiving line, the wedding guests found their tables, and the decibel level fell as people talked with those nearer at hand. There were introductions and handshakes at the mixed tables of artists and Dawes family, as Zoey and Jamie had intended.

I took a moment to check on the kitchen, where Carol Trevett firmly turned me around and sent me back to my seat. It did appear everything was in hand. I made it back to the head table barely in time for my toast.

Pete had discharged his duty the night before. There was no father of the bride to do the honors. Or if there was, he was currently in the medical examiner's office in Augusta. It was on me. I was the one to say what needed to be said.

I stood, raised my glass, and called out until the room quieted. "Welcome to Windsholme and the wedding of Jamie and Zoey," I began. "I have known Jamie for my entire life. He has grown into a loyal, loving, kind, and patient man. He is generous. Many of you here will know how quick he is to lend a hand. He serves honorably in a difficult profession. I love him, and I couldn't wish for a more perfect mate for my friend." I paused to give Jamie his due. A bright beet color rose charmingly from his neck to his hairline.

"Zoey," I pointed my glass in her direction, "is Jamie's perfect match. She is a survivor, but the tough outer shell can't disguise her gooey center. She's a woman who follows her passions and who never, ever gives up on anything, but most especially on the lucky people she loves.

"Join me in wishing them every happiness this life has to offer. I cannot think of two people more deserving." I raised my glass and said, "Here, here." The room echoed it back, even the detectives at the back.

I sat down, grateful to have my last official duty discharged just as the waitstaff arrived with the salad.

Like the rest of the meal, it had been lovingly specified by the bride and groom. Listed on the dinner menu, it was a fennel and blood-orange salad, a favorite of Jamie's. It was served on a plate the color of deep green sea glass. Zoey had made all the dishes for the wedding to complement the food. For this course, she'd also made two little ramekins for each salad. Though the orange, dried cranberries, and dressing were already mixed in, the slivered almonds and blue cheese were served on the side. "Because people can be allergic to nuts," Zoey explained. "And some people don't like blue cheese."

"Some people don't like fennel," Jamie had pointed out. To which Zoey had replied, "Tough."

I was surprised to discover I was starving. I'd picked a little as I'd cleaned up at breakfast but hadn't had a proper meal. I dug into the salad, after emptying the almonds and blue cheese over the top. It was tangly and crispy, crunchy from the nuts and fennel, a perfect blend of flavors. My stomach quieted, though whether that was from at last being filled or from relief that the meal was going so well, I didn't know.

"I love it," Zoey said from beside me. I loved that she loved it.

I liked sitting at the head table, where I could look out across the room. Binder and the detectives were at a hastily added table toward the back. As he'd promised, they ate their salads as any guest would have done. But every time I looked at him, his face and body seemed to be on alert, and his eyes roved around the room.

Tom was at the table with my mom and Captain George, Fee and Vee Snugg, Mr. and Mrs. Gus, and Sonny. He was far more relaxed than his boss, talking and laughing with the others. I felt a warm glow as I watched him, so easy with my family and friends. I never would have believed it when I first met him. He'd been stiff and formal, professional to a fault. And wildly skeptical about my contributions to his investigations. That wasn't the man I watched now. Zoey wasn't the only one with a tough exterior that hid something wonderful inside.

I was momentarily surprised to see that Zoey had put Bill, Constance, Derek, and Amelia at the same table in the middle of the room. Then I realized she'd had no idea about their conflicts back when she'd first arranged the seating chart, or even now. I'd told her about Constance and Kendall Clarkson, but I hadn't said anything about Derek and Bill's unhappy history with him. And I'd persuaded Amelia to remain silent at least for now. Bill and Constance seemed to be talking normally, but Derek glowered, shoveling forks full of salad into his mouth in a mechanical motion. Amelia looked completely miserable, though she managed a tentative smile when she saw me looking. I felt sorry for the four members of Jamie's extended family who had been assigned to fill out the table.

I realized that, while I'd had him, I should have whispered to Tom a quick summary of what I'd learned from Amelia. But, riding the emotions of the day, I couldn't feel bad about the words we'd said instead.

There was a brief interlude when people stretched their legs, headed toward the public restrooms or the bar, or went through the French doors out onto the porch. Despite the fury of the storm the night before, it was sunny, the kind of day, with temps in the mid-seventies, that caused Mainers to brag we didn't need air-conditioning. Which was a lie. Jamie and Zoey went to visit with people at the tables. I curbed a sudden intense desire to check on things in the kitchen. Carol had already dismissed me once.

The waitstaff appeared in the room, banquet trays laden with the main course. We had offered a choice of baked, stuffed lobster tail or beef, or a vegan entrée. I'd been astonished, given the meal the night before, at how many people had ordered lobster again. But some tourists ate lobster every day they were in Maine. I'd often listened as our customers cheerfully described every lobster roll, salad, BLT, bisque, and stew they'd had since they crossed the state line. I had ordered the lobster tail for my own dinner, too. I'd anticipated—correctly, as it turned out—that I wouldn't get any lobster, or food of any kind, at the rehearsal dinner, though I would never in a million years have guessed the reason why.

The tail arrived with the meat standing up like a sail. It sat on a bed of asparagus-mushroom risotto. The plates were a navy-blue color that set off the red of the lobster. "It's beautiful," I said to Zoey. Against the highest odds I could have imagined, her dream wedding was turning out to be just that.

The food was as good as it looked. The lobster, so fresh it had been in cages under our dock that morning, was buttery, luscious, and decadent. I loved the hints of lemon and garlic. The risotto anchored the dish, both physically and on the palate, balancing the briny lobster with the flavor of the spring woods.

I marveled at the amount of work that had gone

into the preparation and presentation. The point was to make the lobster easy for guests in fancy clothing to eat, so I laughed as I looked around at the tables and watched first the Mainers, and then the diners seated with them, say "the heck with it" and go after the meat remaining in the tails with their utensils and, in some cases, their hands.

The dinner plates were scattered with the remnants of the lobster tails when I finally pushed back my chair, no longer hungry. People were moving around again. The detectives had spread out across the room, discreetly drawing guests who'd been at the rehearsal dinner into conversations. Binder had promised they wouldn't bring up the whole man-dying thing during the wedding. Instead, they asked people how they'd liked the party, where they'd sat, who they'd talked with, and so on, making conversation.

My eyes were drawn to the middle of the room, where Constance, Bill, Amelia, and Derek seemed to be having a disagreement. The other three were clearly arguing with Derek, who looked sullen and stubborn. Jordan hovered nearby with drinks on a tray, looking uncertain about whether to interrupt. Drinks were the last thing that table needed.

Outside the room, the DJ cranked up a tune. Jamie and Zoey leapt from their seats, whooped, and ran to the dance floor, and the guests followed.

CHAPTER TWENTY-TWO

Zoey had no father to dance with. I knew for certain that Gus, Captain George, and Jamie's dad had offered, but she had turned them down. Had she been hoping against hope that her father would come? No, that was ridiculous. Those offers had been made weeks before the wedding, before Kendall Clarkson had arrived in town. No one had walked her down the aisle; no one had given her away. "This is me," Zoey was saying. "Take me as I am." Jamie had done just that, and so had his family, whose happy faces and smiling chatter lifted the already buoyant mood.

Immediately after the first dance, Jamie danced with his mom. She had tears in her eyes as he led her around the dance floor. She knew how much he had wanted this. I was certain she'd wondered whether she would ever get this special moment with her youngest son.

The pocket doors from the foyer to the dining room had been opened to create more room for dancing. The DJ was set up in there, and in the corner was the wedding cake. It was white, and traditional, just as Zoey had dreamed. Live flowers spilled from the top and spiraled around the five tiers to the bottom. It sat on a round table on wheels. The plan was that the cake would be wheeled into the foyer to be cut during a break in the dancing.

Were on-duty police detectives allowed to dance? My question was answered when Tom came up behind me, took my hand, and whirled me onto the dance floor as the other guests came pouring on after Jamie's dance. Jamie went straight to Zoey, took her in his arms, and danced away with her. They were both beaming. Tension I hadn't known was there drained from my shoulders so markedly that Tom felt it and smiled at me. His own tension wouldn't end until the killer was caught.

The dance floor filled. Livvie danced with Jack, who lacked in technique, but whose enthusiasm couldn't be questioned. Sonny danced with Page. She looked so grown-up in her purple cocktail dress and high heels, her long, bright red hair pinned up. Sonny beamed, the picture of the proud papa. Tears came to my eyes when I saw them together.

Gus was nowhere in sight. I couldn't imagine the old curmudgeon dancing. Instead, Mrs. Gus, Fee, and Vee formed a merry threesome cutting a rug in a series of imaginative moves.

Mom danced with Captain George, who was surprisingly light-footed for such a big man. George rested an easy hand on her back. I hadn't ever thought they might become engaged and now that it had happened, I was still digesting it. Mom and my dad had been each other's first loves, an improbable romance between a summer girl who lived on a private island and the boy who delivered groceries in his skiff. They were so complementary to each other, so tightly bonded that even after Dad died, it was hard to think of one without the other. Dad had been my mother's best friend. When she'd had him, she needed no other. She'd mourned hard for a long time. But then she'd come back to us, back to her job at the Clambake, and her winter job at Linens and Pantries. Back to the family. Back to her small but treasured circle of friends.

Her relationship with George was different than the one she'd had with my dad. She stood on her own inside it, and so did he. But there was no mistaking that they loved and treasured each other.

George's motivation to marry was even harder to fathom. He'd never been married before, and it seemed late in life to be making that kind of commitment for the first time. Livvie, Page, and I had discussed this ad nauseam. Livvie's theory was that George had been in love with my mother right along, all through the years my parents had run the Clambake and George had piloted the tour boat. George had mourned my father, too, but then time had marched on, and so had he. I absolutely believed, without the slightest bit of evidence, that this was the true story.

George had become a grandfather to Jack, who had never met my dad. George taught Jack how to whistle, skip a stone, and clean a fish. "What do you mean you don't have a captain?" Jack had demanded of a first-grade pal. Until his parents set him straight, he'd believed every kid had one.

"You can declare this wedding a success," Tom said as he danced me to the side of the foyer. "Do you want a drink? I'll get it from the bar."

I wasn't drinking, except for a sip during the champagne toast, but I'd been belting down seltzer waters with lime all evening. Maybe it was time for a real drink. "A rum and tonic, please. While you get it, I'm going to the ladies' room."

I would have preferred to return to my apartment to freshen up, but I was nervous about being off the floor for the time it would take. Instead, I hurried into the public restroom. I walked with my head down, fast, and determined not to be stopped by a request from the staff or a friendly conversation. Without waiting a beat, I pushed open the door of the first stall.

"Excuse me!"

"I'm so sorry."

I had burst in on Constance Marshall, standing in the stall, in the process of giving herself an injection in her belly.

Mortified, I backed up into the sink counter, apologizing the whole way.

Less than a minute later, Constance emerged from the stall. "It's all right, Julia. I should have checked the latch."

"Are you okay?"

She looked back over her shoulder toward the stall. "Oh, that? Yes, fine. I'm used to it. Been doing it for years. I have to be careful when I travel, different time zone, different food, routine all topsy-turvy. But I assure you, I'm fine, just diabetic."

The injection pen had disappeared. Perhaps it was in a case in her slim clutch.

I was glad to escape into the stall as my mind spiraled. We had all assumed the murder was planned because the killer would have had to bring the poison and the means to deliver it to the island. But what if the killing was spontaneous and the murderer had the weapon at hand? Like a syringe and insulin. How much would it take to kill a man? How long would it take to act?

Kendall Clarkson—or Kenneth Clark, as he had called himself then—had hurt Constance deeply and altered the course of her life, in her own telling. Seeing him for the first time in forty years must have been a terrible shock. Her life had recently changed radically with her retirement. Would that destabilize her enough to commit murder? Was I trapped in the bathroom with a killer?

She was still there when I came out of the stall, smiling pleasantly, which comforted me somewhat. "What was going on with Derek at your table?" I asked, making what I hoped was benign conversation. I washed my hands, keeping well back from the sink, careful of my dress and well away from Constance.

"Nothing important," she said. "You don't want to know."

She was right. I didn't. Since I'd put on the light blue gown, the afternoon had enveloped me in a warm cocoon of wedding bliss. I didn't want to deal with the likes of Derek.

"I'm glad to hear—"

That was as far as I got because there was a tremendous crash out on the dance floor, followed by raised voices and another crash.

Constance and I ran out of the room and into the foyer.

Bill Lascelle was on the dance floor, sitting on Derek Quinn, pummeling him mercilessly. Tom attempted to pull Bill off. Jamie knelt beside Derek, shielding the man's body from Bill's blows and taking some of them himself.

Everyone had cleared the dance floor and stood around open-mouthed. Constance was still next to me. "You said this was nothing to worry about," I hissed.

"I didn't think it was. I thought we had it under control."

Zoey found her way to my other side and was making squeaking noises every time Jamie took a punch. I reached for her hand and held on tight. Amelia turned up next to Constance. I thought, over the yelling and the grunting, I heard her making a sound like a growl. I couldn't tell whose side she was on.

Dan Dawes ran across the dance floor. Like many of the men, he'd removed his jacket for the dancing, and he looked like a streak of white as he leapt on the pile. I assumed he had gone to defend his Uncle Jamie, but instead, Dan began drumming Bill with his fists. What on earth did Dan have against Bill Lascelle?

People screamed at the combatants to stop. Women cried. Sonny hoisted a way-too-fascinated Jack on his shoulder firefighter-style and whisked him out the front door. Dan's impact had knocked the pile of thrashing bodies through the archway into the dining room. The DJ reacted by throwing himself over his expensive equipment. Then he took a second look as the fight edged ever closer and ran out of the room.

Several police officers joined in, including the wedding-dressed detectives and Busman's Harbor police who were guests. Uniformed troopers rushed in from outdoors. They grabbed at shirts and limbs, trying to pull people off the pile, but the fight went on.

Zoey's nails dug into my hand so hard it hurt.

They rolled on the floor, punching and grunting. There were so many people involved by that point that I couldn't really see what was happening, but I could see that the ball of human limbs and waving fists was edging ever closer to the table holding the magnificent cake.

Zoey saw it, too. Everyone who wasn't in the fight saw it. There was collective intake of breath.

"Don't!" I shouted along with several others.

The people in the fight didn't hear us and likely couldn't have stopped their momentum anyway. Someone hit the round, wheeled table with a bang.

The cake swayed like a skyscraper in a hurricane, back and forth, and back and forth. The crowd oohed like they were watching a circus trapeze act. The fight stopped. Layers of people jumped off and backed up until only Derek and Bill were left on the floor, looking up, startled. They were on their backs, mouths open, each one with a fistful of the other's shirt.

Jamie and Tom grabbed for the wheeled table,

attempting to stabilize it. The cake briefly righted itself. Then, just as the crowd let out its collective breath, the table rumbled and wobbled. The beautiful cake fell in a perfect arc, tier by tier, the top layers swishing across the dance floor until finally breaking up near the front door. The two big bottom layers fell directly on Derek and Bill, coating them in icing and white cake.

The hall went deathly silent. Carol Trevett ran out of the kitchen, looked at the remains of the beautiful cake, put her hands to her cheeks, and screamed.

CHAPTER TWENTY-THREE

$\mathbf{B}$ill Lascelle sat on the wooden vanity chair in the old billiards room, head in his hands. Even with his face angled downward and covered in icing and cake, I could tell his cheek was already swollen. When he lifted his head, the beginnings of two black eyes were apparent.

"Mr. Lascelle is disinclined to press charges," Lieutenant Binder informed Tom and me as we approached. It felt strange to walk back into the room Mr. Clarkson had so recently vacated.

"I don't want to be involved in some bureaucratic mess here," Bill groaned. "I want to get off this godforsaken island on this godforsaken coast and go home."

"Not to mention avoiding the counterclaims," Tom said, "and possible charges of assaulting an officer." Tom held a dishtowel wrapped around a plastic bag of ice to his forehead. He didn't have the two black eyes, but other than that, he didn't look much better than Bill did.

I'd gathered the plastic bags and towels from

the kitchen and fetched the ice from the new machine behind the bar. Running out of ice was a constant preoccupation on an island where you couldn't get more, though I'd never thought of stocking enough to treat injuries from a fight.

I'd also brought cloths soaked in warm water. I gave one to Bill so that he could begin to get the icing and cake off his face and neck and out of his hair. His suit would have to be dry-cleaned. Or burned.

Bill took the cloth from me and dabbed at his face, gingerly. "That little jerk started it."

"Did you provoke him?" Binder asked.

"No. Of course not. No amount of provocation justifies punching someone in the face. At the wedding of someone you profess to care about, no less. That's not how civilized people behave. Though Derek Quinn can barely be called civilized."

I thought he had a point, at least the "no amount of provocation" part.

"There's been bad blood between you two for years," Tom said. "You may not have started it, but when Quinn gave you the opportunity, you hit back."

"That man robbed me! From the moment I saw his insipid face yesterday afternoon, I wanted to smash it."

"Let's hope he feels the same way about pressing charges that you do," Tom said.

My guess was Derek wanted exactly what Bill wanted, to go home.

"You say he robbed you?" Binder's arms were crossed, his expression serious. Tom must have briefed him on our conversations of the night before, but as the newcomer, he could ask for information previously relayed without appearing to bully or even press.

"It's a long, old story." Lascelle sighed. "I told it to your sergeant last night."

"You told Julia and me it was a long time ago, didn't affect your finances, or your life, and you'd long since gotten past it," Tom reminded him.

"Yeah, well. That's what I tell people, including myself, most of the time. The truth is, it was a terrible time in my life. I was trying to gain a reputation in a completely different space than the one I occupied back then. Bridging two worlds meant I took my eye off the commercial work. My employees lacked supervision, and we'd taken a dive on the creative and the sales side."

"The money did matter," Tom said in a low voice.

"I desperately needed the money. I was elated when every piece in the show sold. I hadn't wanted to have my first serious show in Clarkson's gallery. I thought a more established and prestigious venue would come along. But Derek talked me into it. It was the right offer at the right time. That's the only reason I listened.

"Derek was young and full of himself. He was the worst name-dropper I've ever known. Letting you know he knew this one and that one. A 'name' in every sentence. In my naïvety, even though it was grating, I persuaded myself it was good. Who better to connect you to others than someone who knew everyone? I signed with him. His contacts turned out to be crummy. Kids his age offering 'galleries' that were lofts three flights up with no signage in neighborhoods no sensible person would enter at night—or in the daytime, for that matter. Finally, Derek found Clarkson somewhere. Back then, I imagined it was as much work talking Clarkson into showing me as it was talking me into showing with Clarkson. Derek is a persistent son of a gun. I'll give him that.

"But the show got good notices, and then it was sold out. The theft of the art was never publicized, but the articles about the show, and about the pieces, live on. They're still out there on the internet, linked from my website. That show made my reputation. Though it was hard at the time—I almost lost my business—in the end it was possibly the best thing that has ever happened to me."

What Bill said made sense. Still, it was indisputable. He had hit Derek Quinn. Many times.

Binder was losing his patience. "If it was the best thing that ever happened to you, why the fight with Mr. Quinn?"

"Two reasons," Bill answered. "First, that isn't what started the fight."

That got our attention. "What started the fight?" Tom was mad, and I couldn't blame him. The knot on his forehead was the size of an egg.

"Derek wanted to tell Zoey about her father."

That surprised the three of us into silence.

"She knows about her father," I finally said.

"Not *who* he was," Bill responded. "*What* he was. I don't know the whole story. There were other people at our table. We were talking in low voices, and there were some things I didn't catch. But apparently, Kendall Clarkson did something bad to Derek's girlfriend, Amelia."

"He claimed to be her dad, leached off her, and then stole pretty much everything she had," I informed them.

That brought a raised eyebrow from Binder. "We'll discuss this later," he said to me.

"Constance, Amelia, and I told Derek that saying anything to Zoey was a terrible idea, not the right thing to do on her wedding day. Kendall Clarkson is dead. No further harm can be done. Plus, Amelia said you'd made her promise not to tell Zoey until after the wedding." Bill looked at me, his eyebrows still stuck together with white icing.

"I did," I admitted, which got me an exasperated look from Binder.

"Derek was walking across the dance floor to Zoey. I knew he was going to tell her. I tried to stop him," Bill said. "That's when he hit me."

We'd all seen the aftermath.

"You said there were two things," Tom reminded Bill.

"Ah." Bill put his hands on his knees and leaned forward. It looked like every movement hurt. "The second thing wasn't a direct cause, but it may explain why I was so angry that I responded like I did when Derek hit me. When I'd talked to Clarkson at the cocktail party, the last thing he said to me was that he gave my money to Derek. He insisted Derek was the one who never paid me."

"And you believed him?" I didn't believe it.

"I'm not a fan of either one of them, to tell the truth. Does it make a difference? Derek was my agent. He was supposed to vet the gallery owner. He was supposed to handle the contract and the money. I don't know which one took the money and which one took the art, but they're both guilty, as far as I'm concerned."

Binder dropped his arms to his sides and took a wider stance, as if digging in. "You slugged Mr. Quinn, demonstrating you aren't opposed to violence. Did you kill Mr. Clarkson?"

"No!"

"Do you think Mr. Quinn murdered Mr. Clarkson?" Binder's tone was grave, and his eyes drilled into Bill's face.

"I have no reason to know one way or another. Look, I love Zoey. I've never married or had children. I look at Zoey and a few others I've mentored over the years as my legacy, as important as my art. I have never seen her as happy as she was at the wedding rehearsal. No matter my personal feelings, I would never, ever jeopardize that. As it is, what's happened breaks my heart."

It broke my heart, too.

"You're free to go when the tour boat leaves, Mr. Lascelle," Binder said. "One of my detectives will escort you upstairs so you can get cleaned up and change. He'll take your contact information."

Bill rose laboriously to his feet. I wondered if a rib was broken. "You keep that jerk away from me."

"Don't worry," Binder said as Bill started toward the door, moving slowly. "We will."

"I understand why Derek hit you," I called to him. "And why you hit Derek. But why was Dan Dawes punching you?"

Bill's brows rose, cracking the dried icing still smeared across his forehead. "I have absolutely no idea."

One of the detectives waited for Bill in the doorway. Another would bring Derek into the billiards room, but after a delay, so there was no chance the men would cross paths. I used the time to fill Tom and Binder in on what Amelia had told me about

Clarkson in the most condensed version I could manage.

"Definitely a scam," Tom said when I finished.

"Probably a scam. The DNA test was never analyzed. Amelia desperately wants Zoey to be her sister."

Binder grunted. "If wishes were horses . . ."

"Yeah," Tom agreed.

"There's something else." I told them about my encounter with Constance in the ladies' room. "Could the murder weapon have been insulin?"

"Could be." Tom took his phone from his pocket. He'd given up on the ice. The egg on his forehead had a purplish cast. He stepped through the French doors to the porch to look for a place to call the medical examiner.

Derek entered through the door from the main salon, escorted by the female detective. "Mr. Quinn, if you would have a seat." Binder indicated the wooden chair. He sounded polite, but there was nothing of a suggestion about it.

Like Bill, Derek looked the worse for wear. He'd wiped as much cake and icing off his face as he could, but most of the bottom tier of the cake seemed to have landed in his lap. His lower lip was split. The vertical line of oozing red looked nasty. I was relieved none of the injuries appeared to be truly serious. There was no medical care on the island. Even if one of the guests turned out to be a doctor, I could provide nothing beyond our first-aid kit.

"Tell me what that was all about." Binder pointed in the general direction of the foyer and dining room.

"Do I have to?"

"Let me see." Binder met attitude with attitude. "Your friend Mr. Lascelle isn't interested in pressing charges. I, however, have injured officers. I can approach the prosecutor about several serious allegations. Would you like me to do that?"

Derek was chastened. "No."

"Are you interested in bringing countercharges against Mr. Lascelle or anyone else involved?" Binder asked.

"*No.*"

"Good. I return to my original request. Tell us what happened in there."

Derek took a deep breath. "Specifically, what happened is Bill got in my face."

Tom came back into the room. "ME's out. Will call back," he murmured.

"Please expand." Binder motioned with his hand for Derek to go on.

Derek inhaled again. "Bill and I had a difference of opinion. I wanted to tell Zoey something. He didn't want me to. When he saw me walking over to Zoey, he tried to stop me. I was only going to ask her to dance! I didn't like him telling me what to do. Or what not to do. I asked him to move aside. He declined. I popped him one."

"What was it you wanted to tell the bride?" Binder asked.

Derek told almost the same story Bill had, except in this version, Derek had decided against telling Zoey during the wedding about what had happened to Amelia.

"What changed your mind?" Tom seemed only mildly interested.

"They changed my mind. Bill, Constance, and

Amelia. Amelia said you made her promise." Derek glared at me.

Had I caused this scene? In my zeal to protect Zoey, had I inadvertently set the fight between Bill and Derek in motion? Maybe if I had just let Amelia tell? I shook my head. No, that was wrong. It was Zoey's day.

"I think Zoey should know. But not today. I would never want to hurt her." Derek dropped his eyes and said, in a voice barely above a whisper, "I love her."

We were all silent for a moment, acknowledging that. Not that it was news to anyone in the room, but we had to give Derek his due.

Binder decided it was time to move on. "You and Mr. Lascelle have had a problem with each other for a long time, having to do with the ceramic show at Kendall Clarkson's gallery."

"Yes," Derek agreed, "having to do with that."

"Lascelle was never paid," Tom stated.

"Neither was I! We were both ripped off by that old man. It's old news," Derek insisted. "Past history. Water under the bridge. Or over the dam. Wherever water goes."

"Mr. Quinn, did you kill Mr. Clarkson?" Binder asked.

"No."

"Do you think Bill Lascelle killed Mr. Clarkson?"

Derek attempted a shrug that ended in a wince. "How would I know?"

Binder continued. "Before he died, did Mr. Clarkson say anything to you to renew your anger toward Mr. Lascelle?"

Derek appeared genuinely baffled. "When, yesterday? I never talked to him. I never went near the guy. The last thing I wanted was to talk to Kendall Clarkson, especially after I realized Bill was here."

Despite my dislike for the man, I was inclined to believe him.

Binder told Derek the same things he'd told Bill. He could leave on the boat, a detective would escort him to his room, and so on. And to stay far, far away from Bill Lascelle.

I wanted to tell him to stay away from Zoey and Amelia too, but I didn't have a badge.

Derek rose, slowly. He stuck his hand out to the lieutenant. The knuckles were puffy and red. Binder took it, very carefully, and shook. The female detective appeared, and Derek was gone.

"Where's Dawes?" Binder asked.

"I imagine he's with Zoey," I said.

"Not *Jamie* Dawes, Daniel Dawes. The one who was beating up Lascelle."

"He's sitting out on the porch," Tom said, "having a smoke."

"Bring him in, please."

Dan walked into the old billiards room, looking relaxed. His tuxedo jacket was still off. He was also barefoot. Of everyone involved in the fracas I had seen so far, he seemed to be hurting the least and had avoided all but a few splatters of cake.

"What's up?" he asked as Tom offered him the wooden chair. "No, thanks. I'll stand." He seemed more curious than alarmed.

"Why did you join in the fight?" Binder asked.

"Lots of people did. I thought I could help out."

"Help out?" Tom's voice was probably louder than he intended. He took a quick look around the otherwise empty room and lowered it. "I was in that pile. You weren't pulling people off. You were whaling on Bill Lascelle."

Dan's open features crinkled into a frown. "You saw that? I'm afraid I lost my temper." Dan looked from Tom to Binder and back. "Is Lascelle saying he'll press charges?"

"No," Binder answered without elaborating. "Was your temper provoked by your part in Kendall Clarkson's art swindle ten years ago? I understand you were the victim."

"*One* of the victims."

"You mean that Derek Quinn and Bill Lascelle were also victims?" I asked, interested.

"I mean the art at that show was sold several times over. There were at least three other buyers I was able to track down. None of the people I found actually got delivery. I assumed someone did, but I've never been able to find the pieces. As far as I know, they've never been seen again."

"Why did you seek out the others?" I was merely curious. I didn't think any of the other buyers would have randomly traveled to our little corner of the universe to murder Kendall Clarkson.

"At one point, I considered a lawsuit," Dawes answered. "But as I met with them, I realized it wasn't going to happen."

"Why not?" Binder asked.

"They were genuinely rich people. The money was a drop in the bucket for them. They were more angry because they'd been embarrassed than because they'd lost money. The last thing they wanted was to have it all out in public. After due consideration, publicity was the last thing I wanted, too."

"But *you're* a genuinely rich person," Tom pointed out.

"I wasn't then. When you start a company that gets significant investment, you aren't instantly rich. You have a lot of money on paper as the value of the company goes up with each round of financing, but you don't have cash. In fact, you're urged to take as little cash out of the company as possible. The money is meant to grow the business."

From my work in venture capital, I knew exactly what he was talking about. Dan seemed to sense that and addressed the rest of his answer to me. "I told you I bought the art to decorate our new headquarters—"

"You bought the art with company money," I guessed.

He blushed, embarrassed even after all this time, even after his early investors had made back their money many times over. "It was such a rookie mistake. Not only had I spent money meant for office furniture, equipment, and the like on art, I didn't have the art to show for it. If I'd had the ceramics, believe me, I would have sold them to one of those other interested parties as soon as I came to my senses. As it was, I stopped taking a salary until the money was made up. I had to move back in with my folks, but it was worth it."

Being swindled by Clarkson wasn't the little deal Dan had made it out to be. His board would have looked negatively on the expenditure, even if it had gone as expected. It might not have been enough to get him fired or defunded, especially if the investors still had hopes he'd make them a pile

of money, but if they'd begun to doubt that out-
come, it would have been a quick excuse to get rid
of him. And he hadn't said how he'd accounted
for the money he'd returned. Perhaps he'd confessed to his board and worked it off. If he'd done
it any other way, like sneaking salary money back
into the equipment account, it would be an even
bigger deal, possibly a crime.

"Did that make you want to kill Kendall Clarkson?" Binder asked.

Dan looked startled, almost as if, with the wedding and the fight, he'd forgotten what this was all
about. "Maybe at the time. Not for revenge, but
out of fear. And anger at myself for my own stupid-
ity. But it's been over for some time. At least I
thought it was."

"Then why beat Bill Lascelle and not Derek
Quinn?" Tom asked.

Dan blinked. "Who is Derek Quinn?"

"The guy on the bottom of the pile." Tom pointed
to the floor of the billiards room. It was original to
the house, the same oak as in the foyer and dining
room.

"That guy. I saw him around yesterday and
today, mostly eyeing my uncle's bride like she was a
Delmonico steak. We were never introduced. I didn't
know his name."

"But you recognized Lascelle," Binder said.

"We were introduced today before the ceremony."
Dan stopped talking for a moment. His bare toes
dug into the floorboards. "But he'd been pointed
out to me last night . . . by Kendall Clarkson."

"You told my colleague," Binder nodded toward
Tom, "that you and Clarkson talked about sports."

"Yes, well. Not entirely. As the meal went on and

he was eating his chowder and talking to my dad as if nothing had ever happened between him and me, I got madder and madder. I couldn't stop myself. I got his attention away from my dad and confronted him as quietly as I could manage. The story poured out of me. I told him he had come close to ruining my life.

"Clarkson wasn't ruffled. He claimed we were both victims. He said Bill Lascelle had come to the gallery, collected the money, and promised to deliver the artwork. Lascelle had said that, given the fragility of the pieces, he was the only one who could pack them, move them, and install them. Clarkson told me he never saw Lascelle, the money, or the ceramics again."

"Did you believe him?" I asked.

Dan shook his head. "Of course not. For one thing, there were the other buyers. I wanted to push that back in his face, but then the waiter showed up with his drink, and the next thing I knew, Clarkson was on the floor gasping for air."

"But when the fight started today . . ." Binder prompted.

"When I saw that other guy hitting Lascelle, I swear my brain left my body. I saw red, and I jumped into the fray." He turned to me. "I'm sorry."

Of the people in the room, I supposed I was the one most owed an apology. But if any of his blows had landed on Tom, he might have the greater claim. Beyond us, I thought there were people who deserved an apology much more.

"Mr. Dawes," Binder said, "did you murder Kendall Clarkson?"

Dan's brows shot up. "What? I've never murdered anyone, and I never would."

CHAPTER TWENTY-FOUR

"Could any of what Clarkson told either Lascelle or Dawes be true?" Binder asked.

I shook my head, but it was Tom who spoke. "Clarkson was a bad guy, a scammer of artists, a user of vulnerable women, all his life. If his mouth was moving, he was lying. He was stirring up trouble right to the end, as it turned out."

I didn't disagree. Though I was sorry he was murdered, and especially about the time and place, it was hard to argue that the world wasn't better off without Kendall Clarkson. However awful this whole mess had been, he hadn't gotten to complete what turned out to be his final scam on my friend. Speaking of whom, I needed to get back to my bridesmaid duties.

"Nothing from the ME?" Binder asked Tom.

Tom looked at his phone and shook his head. "I'll call again."

He headed out the door, Binder went to find the rest of the team, and I went in search of Zoey.

As I passed through the main salon, I was happy

to see the catering team had put out coffee, and in
lieu of the ruined cake, the chocolate-covered tof-
fee squares and other snacks, sweet and savory,
we'd planned to serve before the guests boarded
the *Jacquie II* for home.

Most people had scattered to Windsholme's big
front porch and the lawn. I hoped the din of conversation coming from out there meant they were
recovering from our most recent drama.

The DJ had put on some calming, light music.
When I passed the entrance to the dining room, a
longtime member of our waitstaff was mopping
the floor. I called out a heartfelt thank-you, more
grateful than ever for good employees and good
contractors who knew what to do and kept everything running as smoothly as they could.

When I checked in the kitchen, the uniformed
state troopers were eating with the waitstaff amid
much joking and hilarity. The caterers were packing their plastic containers with every bottle and
jar and piece of equipment they'd brought to the
island, preparing to load them onto the *Jacquie II*
when it was time to go.

Jordan was in the corner of the kitchen, talking
to the tall woman who was packing a box with
spice jars. He cast a look over his shoulder. "Julia,
come and meet my mom!" He came to the center
of the room and dragged me toward her. I hadn't
seen it before, but when I looked at the two side by
side, the resemblance was obvious. They had the
same sandy-colored brows and widely spaced eyes.
I didn't think the woman's hair was so dark naturally.

"Mrs. Thomas, I'm so pleased to meet you." I
put out my hand.

She took it. "Same. I'm Mel."

"Thank you so much for all you've done here today under what I'm sure were the most difficult circumstances. The food was amazing. Jamie and Zoey are thankful, and so am I."

"That's lovely of you to say."

She didn't say anything else, so I went on. "If there's anything I can do to help you get settled in, don't hesitate to ask." They'd need more than her catering job to get through the winter. "In the fall, maybe I can suggest some places for you and Jordan to apply for work."

"Thanks. I'm not sure we'll be here then. We haven't decided. We're playing it by ear."

I was surprised. I could tell by his look that Jordan was surprised, too. He'd made the move sound permanent when he spoke to me. But Maine winters weren't for everyone. Perhaps the cold spring in a tent had given his mother second thoughts.

"Excuse me," I said. "I have to find the bride."

Zoey was in my apartment. Eloise was tidying her hair and reapplying her makeup. Livvie was there, and so was Amelia. Zoey was smiling into the mirror.

I rushed to her. "I am so sorry."

Her smile grew even bigger, and then she laughed. "Don't be. This has turned out to be a wedding no one will ever forget." She could tell I wasn't convinced. "Honestly, Julia, we'll laugh about that cake someday."

The mood in the room was decidedly upbeat. I

let out a long breath I felt like I'd been holding since the fight.

"I told Zoey about our father," Amelia said. "Our possible father. You asked me to wait until after the wedding, but I thought the wedding might be over, and I didn't want to miss the chance."

Zoey reached over and took Amelia's hand. "Don't move!" Eloise hissed.

"Isn't it exciting that we might be sisters?" Zoey looked from Livvie to me and back. "I've always been jealous of you two."

Amelia was beaming. I'd known Zoey would be kind. I didn't know whether to root for Kendall Carson to be their father or root for him not to be. I just hoped there wasn't another disappointment ahead for the two of them.

"What do you want to do?" I asked Zoey. "I can tell Captain George to start the *Jacquie II*'s engines and send these people home." The ceremony and meal were over. We'd managed to meet the main goals of the day.

"Absolutely not!" Zoey answered. "It's my wedding day. We're going to get this back on track. Next, I'm going to throw the bouquet. And, Julia and Amelia, you're going to be downstairs, trying to catch it."

Through almost twenty years of single life, I had never been a fan of that particular tradition, but if Zoey wanted it, we were going to do it. Eloise finished applying Zoey's lipstick, brushed some power on her nose, and we stood to go.

Zoey stopped on the lower landing of the grand staircase overlooking the foyer, a perfect balcony. I called everyone to order, chasing them from the porch, the lawn, and the main salon. Zoey looked dramatic up there as she urged for the single women to gather. She motioned Amelia and me out on the floor, where we joined the others. Fee and Vee invariably took part in this ritual, making exaggerated reaching and pushing motions that always got a laugh. My mother stood in the ring of spectators. She never, ever would have participated, even in the years after my father died and before Captain George came along. She smiled at me encouragingly.

Zoey wound up and whipped the bouquet right at me, overhand. I put my hands up to protect my face, and the flowers landed in my arms. "You're next!" she shouted, and everyone cheered.

I smiled as graciously as I could, the good sport, but the voice in my head cynically chirped, *fat chance.* There was no wedding on the horizon. Then I remembered the theoretical conversation about the theoretical wedding with Tom the night before. But, as I knew, theoretical conversations don't always become real ones.

Everyone applauded, and the DJ, bless him, put on a rousing tune. Zoey flew down the stairs and into Jamie's arms to lead the dancing. The rest of the crowd joined in enthusiastically, and the foyer and dining room thundered with the sounds of shouts and whoops and dancing feet.

Tom appeared from somewhere, looked at the bouquet, and raised his eyebrows wordlessly. He took the flowers from me, leaned in, and kissed me. "I have to work," he said. "I'm sorry."

"I know. I wouldn't have it any other way."

An hour later, Binder's detectives moved through the crowd, collecting contact information for everyone who had been at the rehearsal dinner. Zoey had their addresses, already written out on the envelopes that would contain her thank-you notes. She probably had their phone numbers and emails too, except perhaps for a few plus-ones, but the police had their procedures.

The detectives' movement through the crowd had the effect of breaking up the party. The French doors were still open, though the evening was getting cooler. People gathered in the main salon, talking, picking up the centerpieces they'd won by having the closest birthday, snacking on the cookies. No one mentioned the murder or the fight. I was sure they'd talk of nothing else when they got on the boat, but for now, they were being respectful to Zoey and Jamie.

The bar was closed. We'd run out of liquor, something I'd never expected. The bartender offered to run down to the dining pavilion and collect the bottles there, but I nixed it. Enough was enough. Besides, we were out of ice.

Tom and Binder were in the billiards room, quietly discussing their next steps. Tom was beyond exhausted, and Binder was clearly deflated by the prospect of losing all his witnesses and suspects to the real world.

"The medical examiner called back," Tom told me, when I sat in one of the satiny chairs and took off my shoes. "He won't know what killed Clarkson until the lab work comes back. That will be days. But he did say that our corpse died from an injection of a poisonous substance; we just don't know which one. It was a murder. He also said that, based on my description of what happened after Clarkson fell off the bench, it wasn't likely to have been insulin. Much more likely, but certainly not definitely, it was nicotine."

"Then not Constance Marshall." I was relieved. I liked Constance.

"Not Constance Marshall with *insulin*," Binder corrected.

"The ME also said if it was nicotine, it wouldn't have acted instantly. It would have been administered twenty to thirty minutes before to have that affect." Tom looked at each of us to make sure we'd understood the significance of that.

"So not Dan or Jordan," I said. I liked them, too.

"Not Dan or Jordan at the picnic table." Binder was beginning to irritate me, but he wasn't wrong. "Either one of them could have done it before."

"No one saw Dan Dawes anywhere near our victim during the cocktail party," Tom reminded him. "Jordan was serving drinks. He might have been near Clarkson."

"I did see Jordan near Clarkson, when he served a drink to Bill," I said. "How much would a needle like that hurt? The hole was tiny."

Tom knew the answer. "The ME said, based on the size, it probably felt to Clarkson like a bee sting."

Something shimmered in my mind, a remembered moment I couldn't quite catch. "When did Clarkson last get out of prison?"

Binder squinched up his face, remembering. "Just over a year ago. He did eighteen months for writing some bad checks to an elderly woman for some antique paintings. Clarkson wouldn't have got that much if it weren't for his priors."

"Here's what we know about Kendall Clarkson," I said, ticking on my fingers. "One, he's a con man.

He seems prone to art cons, and that's what he's gone to prison for. Two, when he's out of prison, he takes advantage of vulnerable women. Three, he's been out of his last stint in prison for over a year. Where's he been? What's he been doing?"

"Attempting to con Zoey," Tom answered. "Though only lately."

"I think he saw articles about Zoey's success online. He did some research, found her wedding announcement, decided to come here."

"Makes sense," Binder said.

"He didn't seem to care if his previous victims were successful," Tom argued. "Constance Marshall was at the beginning of her teaching career, had very little money. Zoey's mother worked as a waitress. Amelia Gerhart didn't have much money, either. She's a kid."

"Agreed," I said. "Their lack of resources and maybe a related lack of confidence made them vulnerable."

"We don't know where Clarkson's been," Binder said. "He served his full term this last time. No parole. No parole officer to keep track of him."

Tom saw where I was going. "He's been living with a woman. And robbing her."

Binder was unconvinced. "It had to have been someone who was here last night. And someone who knew Clarkson would be here because whoever it was brought the nicotine and the syringe. That makes it much more likely it's someone we've already spoken to. Not a mystery woman."

"Not a mystery woman," I said.

CHAPTER TWENTY-FIVE

Tom went upstairs to collect the clothes he'd worn to the rehearsal dinner. Binder was rounding up his detectives. I went to find Jordan Thomas.

He was in the kitchen, his back to me, packing one of the last plastic totes for the boat. He was alone. The caterers were carrying their stuff and the day's garbage down to the *Jacquie II*, helped by the waitstaff and even some of the uniformed police who were clocking off duty.

"Jordan, I need to talk to you." I kept my voice as even as I could.

He turned around, his face in a worried frown. "Did I do something wrong? If I did, I'm sorry. I'm learning." He held out his arms in a gesture of hopelessness.

"You did great." I said. "Jordan, tell me why you're not in school."

His face fell, and he didn't speak for a long time. "How much do you know?" he finally asked.

"Very little. Start from the beginning."

He looked around, as if he might be rescued

from a conversation he profoundly did not want to have by the arrival of another person. Then he groaned, putting both hands to his face. "It was always just my mom and me," he began, his hands falling to his sides. "And that was fine. She's a great mom. I never felt the lack of anything. Really. Maybe on Parents Day at school, or at Boy Scouts, but hardly ever."

"What did your mother tell you about your father?"

"Almost nothing. I didn't like to ask. It made her unhappy, and I tried my hardest not to make her unhappy." He stopped speaking. I thought he might refuse to continue, but then he started again. "Because we were so tight, when I went away to college last August, it was hard for Mom. Not that she didn't want me to go. It was all she ever talked about, going to a good school, getting a good start in life. But I'm sure she was lonely. Taking care of me had been a big part of her life. The biggest part."

He breathed deeply to steady himself. We were coming to the heart of the story. "Like I said, I left for school in August for freshman stuff. I was at UC Davis. I loved it and was doing well in my classes. I made friends. I missed Mom for sure, and probably I could have checked in more, though I don't think it would have made a difference. When I came home for Thanksgiving, there was this guy living in our house."

"Kendall Clarkson."

"Yes. But he called himself Kent Carlson." Jordan squared his shoulders and went on. "I didn't like him. I didn't like him one bit. But I told myself it was none of my business. Mom had dedicated her life to me for eighteen years. She should be able to find her own happiness. I thought I was jealous, and that was a pretty immature way to be. So I kept my mouth shut. I went back to school for my finals."

He paused and looked around again, still hoping help might come in the form of an interruption. I was pretty certain it wouldn't. The kitchen was clean, its surfaces empty and shining. If the merry band of caterers, servers, and troopers had taken the last loads to the boat, they would have stayed on it or down near the dock.

"When I went back for Christmas, I was relieved the guy was gone. My mother said only that they broke up. I figured she'd come to her senses. At least that what I wished."

He paused, and I thought of what Binder had said, "If wishes were horses . . ."

"Things were a little odd at home. The tree wasn't up, or any decorations, no lights outside. Mom is a hard-core Christmas person. The decorations normally would have gone up the Monday after Thanksgiving. I'd brought the boxes up from the basement when I was home, but that was as far as she got. I rationalized that she'd been distracted with the breakup, and she didn't have me at home to appreciate the tree. I thought maybe that, all those years, the decorations were for me and not something she loved to do, like she'd often told me."

Jordan's voice was steady. It might be a relief to be finally telling this story.

"Mom told me she'd taken vacation from work for my entire time off so that we could hang out together," he continued. "That seemed extreme to me. I had high school friends I wanted to spend time with. But I was so glad that guy was out of the picture I didn't object. I didn't see what was clearly in front of my face."

He was sad and worried, but there was a good measure of guilt in him, too. Even though I hadn't yet heard the full story, I wanted to hug the poor kid and tell him that it was Kendall Clarkson who was guilty, not him. Instead, I asked, "What did your mother do for work?"

"She worked at an animation studio. She started as a storyboard artist soon after I was born, but now she manages lots of people. She's not an executive, but almost."

Another artist. "Did she say how she met Clarkson, er, Carlson?"

He gave me a fleeting smile. "I know who you're talking about. In a museum. They were admiring the same painting."

I nodded; that certainly tracked with Clarkson's MO.

Jordan continued. "I went back to school. It was two weeks into the winter quarter when I got called into the bursar's office. They told me I couldn't continue with my classes because my tuition hadn't been paid. My dorm fees hadn't been paid either. I was sure it was a mistake. I called Mom, but she didn't answer. I texted and emailed. I even called her work. The person who picked up told me Mom was out sick."

My stomach curled into a knot; even though I'd been expecting this story, listening to the pain and confusion that still lingered in Jordan's voice was gutting.

"Finally, I reached her. She sounded funny. She said I needed to come home. I was already packed.

I'd been so worried. I took a bus. It was sixteen panicking hours. When I got to the house, it was dark. No lights were on. She told me that, when Carlson had gone, he'd taken all her money—savings, retirement fund, my college fund, everything. He'd maxed out her credit cards. She couldn't pay them off, and her credit was being destroyed. He even took her car."

Clarkson had finally found a mark who had money.

"Mom wasn't up to going to work. She pretty much stayed in bed all day and watched television all night. Her employer was patient; she'd been there forever, but eventually they had to put her on unpaid leave. I begged her to go to a doctor. I thought maybe then she could go on disability from work, but she totally refused.

"I got jobs at two restaurants, the ones I gave you for references. I made enough to keep us fed and keep the lights on, but I couldn't make enough for the mortgage. We'd moved right before high school to get closer to the private school I attended. Our house was really nice, but expensive."

He had painted a picture for me. A very sad picture. But something must have changed.

"One day, I got home from work and Mom was up." Jordan smiled at the memory. "There was laundry in the washer and dinner on the table. Mom is a great cook. She's taken lots of classes and stuff. That's how she got the job with Ms. Trevett after a tryout. Again, I should have realized something was up, but I was so happy to have her back, I didn't probe too much."

"Stop blaming yourself," I said. "You didn't cause this."

"I sort of did. If I hadn't been born, Mom wouldn't be, well, who she is. She'd have had a different life. Maybe even a nice husband and other kids. And even with the life we had, if I hadn't left for college, she wouldn't have brought that man home."

"Your mother doesn't wish you weren't born," I said firmly. "That's the last thing she wishes. And you said yourself her greatest hope was for you to go to college." I looked into his eyes to see if he believed me. I saw a flicker of relief, perhaps, but then the sadness and the guilt returned. "When did your mother start feeling better?"

"It was the end of March. I didn't expect it to last, but it did. She was up every day, showered and dressed. She didn't go back to work, but otherwise she was her old self. A week later, she told me not to pay the utilities and the minimum payments I'd been making on the credit cards, hoping maybe to get some of her credit back. Mom said that, instead, we were going to save my cash tips and convert my checks to cash so we could take a cross-country trip. She'd agreed to trade some of our good furniture to a neighbor for a used car. I was surprised, but happy to play along if she was smiling."

It wasn't until two days before they left that Mel Thomas told her son they weren't coming back; they were moving to Maine permanently. She'd always wanted to live on a craggy coast. He should pack not only clothes, but his scrapbook and the bear he'd slept with as a child and any other favored remembrances because the sheriff would surely be seizing the house in their absence.

This struck me as disordered thinking. The house was probably worth more than she'd paid and would have sold quickly in a hot Los Angeles real estate market. I wondered if Jordan was sophisticated enough to realize this. He'd had to grow up quickly in the last few months, but he'd been a freshman in college when the whole ordeal began. Probably not much interested in mortgages or home buying. He did know, he told me, that there were craggy coasts a lot closer than Maine but had been so grateful to have his mother back, he didn't argue.

The trip across country hadn't quite been the adventure she'd sold him. They had some fun and saw some sights, but by the time they left Memphis, they barely had enough money for food and gas. They slept in their car, so they'd have money for the deposit when they got to the campground. As to why Busman's Harbor, he hadn't understood that until today, when the pieces of the puzzle had fallen into place for him.

"I agreed to come here to start a new life for both of us," he finished, his breath ragged. "That's all it ever was to me." He stopped talking abruptly, like a machine that had been unplugged.

"And now you're worried your mother killed Kendall Clarkson." I looked directly into his eyes.

But instead of looking at me, his eyes grew wide, like he couldn't believe what he was seeing. His mouth opened, but no sound came out.

I whirled around to see Mel Thomas advancing on me, a big kitchen knife in her fist, aimed at my neck. I leapt sideways as the knife whooshed past me. I was fast, but Jordan was faster. His hand shot out toward the blade of the knife just as his mother brought it down.

He screamed as a line of red spread across his

palm, and then blood ran down his hand, dripping from his fingers onto the floor.

The knife dropped with a clatter, and Jordan's mom sank to her knees. She pulled her son down to her until his head was in her lap. She held up the bloody hand, applying pressure and looked at me in desperation. "Do something. Do something. Please."

Jordan whimperéd. His mother sobbed. I kicked the knife across the floor, far out of her reach, and then yelled for help as loudly as I could.

Mel Thomas sat on a stool in the kitchen, her hands cuffed behind her back.

Tom had been the first one through the door. When he'd seen Mel and Jordan on the floor, Jordan bleeding on the white and black tiles, he yelled for others to help.

Now Jordan was on another stool about ten feet from his mother. The same state trooper who had put the plastic ties around his mother's wrists had bandaged his wound. "Good enough until we can him get to a hospital," he'd said. The first-aid kit had finally been good for something.

Binder had offered to have the trooper take Jordan to another part of the house to wait, but the boy had refused. He was staying with his mother until he couldn't anymore.

"Let him stay." Binder said. The trooper went away.

That left the five of us, Jordan, his mother, Binder, Tom, and me. The long June twilight had finally ended. It was fully dark outside, but the kitchen was brightly lit. Binder had let the *Jacquie ll* go back to town. Livvie had taken her children to the little yellow house. Sonny had ferried the bride and groom to Busman's Harbor. They'd spend the night in Zoey's apartment. Binder had said he would interview them in the morning so they could leave on their honeymoon, delayed only by a few hours.

Tom pulled three more stools from under the stainless-steel table, and we sat about ten feet away, facing Jordan and his mother in their corners.

"I wouldn't have killed you," Mel said to me. She turned to her son. "I never meant to hurt you. I don't mean just that." She pointed to his hand, and then she cried.

"But you did mean to kill Kendall Clarkson," Binder said when she quieted, his tone neutral, the statement of a fact.

I widened my eyes at Jordan from the other side of the room and jerked my head toward his mother. Tom had read her the Miranda warning when they'd put the handcuffs on her. She'd responded, but I wasn't sure she'd taken it in.

Jordan understood me and said, "Mom, you should wait for a lawyer."

Mel shook her head so hard she nearly fell off the stool, her balance diminished by the hands tied behind her back. "No." She was definite. "I want to tell. I want people to know what happened to me."

Tom waved his phone at her and pantomimed pushing the record button. She nodded her assent. He stood and put it on the stainless-steel table at the corner nearest her.

"I met him in September, Clarkson—or Carlson, as he was calling himself then—at the Getty. I often went there for inspiration for my work, but that day I was filling up an empty Saturday afternoon. Jordan had always played soccer, and that had taken up my fall weekends for more than a decade. I was very much at a loss. I was admiring a still life by Cezanne, a bowl filled with apples, when Kent came up beside me and we began to chat. He was so knowledgeable about the painting and the artist. I was charmed immediately. He was handsome and well-dressed." She looked at me for a female opinion. Clarkson was good-looking, and the blue blazer had fit him like it was custom-tailored.

I nodded my confirmation, and she went on. "If he was a little older, so be it. We went out for coffee and the next time for dinner, and then he stayed over one night and then another. I had never had men over when Jordan was home. It was intoxicating.

"I assumed, in the beginning, that he had his own place, and we were spending lots of time at mine. But bits and pieces began to appear in my house, clothing, and grooming stuff at first. Then paints and canvases in various stages of completion. He took over my sunroom. Then he brought in finished ceramics and paintings by other artists. I finally realized, 'Oh, he's living here.'"

She stopped for a moment and asked for a glass of water. Tom fetched it from the sink and held it to her lips as she drank. "That's enough. Thanks." She started again. "I'd thought, when we met and for weeks afterward, that he was retired. He didn't go out to work. That much was clear. Slowly, I became aware that he hadn't offered to pay for anything.

"These things put me off, but when Jordan came home for Thanksgiving, I introduced them. Kent was living in the house and had nowhere else to go, so there wasn't any choice about it. Nevertheless, I'd never had Jordan meet any man I'd dated before. It felt like a big deal. A rite of passage.

"Then, two days after Jordan left, Kent was gone. And so was every penny I had. But you'll already know that part of the story."

I did, and Tom and Binder knew enough about Kendall Clarkson to guess.

"I was stunned. I was angry, but most of all, I was hurt." Her face drew up in a terrible grimace that I thought would become a sob, but it didn't. Instead, she exhaled loudly and continued. "I started to miss work. Kent had taken my car, and my savings, any hope of buying another car. I was Ubering to work on the days I could get it together enough to go in. When they canceled my credit cards, even that wasn't possible. Days at a time, I would lie in my bed with the covers over my head.

"I spent a lot of my time speculating about what kind of person Kent was. How I, a mature woman with some experience with men, had been completely taken in by him. I went over every moment of our brief courtship, and then our domestic life. I stalked him on the internet, but he'd given me a false name. I kept looking, looking, looking for the hints. For the tells. What did I miss?

"I'd missed so many things I came to see clearly in retrospect. But my romantic hurt wasn't the worst of it. I'd always, always taken inordinate pride in how well I, a single parent, had provided for Jordan and me. We were financially stable. I could cover most of Jordan's college expenses. I'd saved for my retirement. When Kent took that, I couldn't recover. We were in financial free fall. Even worse, my identity as a competent, self-sufficient woman who could care for her fatherless child was exploded. Kendall Clarkson had robbed me of my identity as a mother, as an employee, and as a person. I didn't know who I was anymore. I felt like a ghost."

"Mom." Jordan's voice was ragged with emotion. "You were the best mom anyone ever had."

"You never reported this to the police," Tom said.

Mel shrugged her shoulders as much as she was able to with her hands cuffed behind her back. "I was embarrassed. And what would I have told them? As it turned out, I didn't even know his name."

She swallowed and went on. "Later, I remembered a conversation with Kent about his daughter," Mel said. "He never spoke about family, but that one time he bragged about how successful she was. Playing the proud papa, or maybe actually being one. He let down his guard, and her name had slipped out. Zoey Butterfield.

"I stalked her on the web, inhaling everything I could find. I put an alert on her name, and at the end of March, delivered to my inbox, was a link to a newspaper in Busman's Harbor, Maine. It announced the wedding of Zoey Butterfield to James Dawes, on Morrow Island, the first weekend in June. At last, I had a reason to get up in the morning. I convinced Jordan to move across the country."

She stopped abruptly, as if she'd only in that

moment realized what she'd said. "I'm sorry, honey. It was wrong of me to involve you even in the most tangential way. But I couldn't leave you behind. You were all I had left."

Jordan's brown eyes shimmered with tears that didn't fall. He gulped, his Adam's apple moving up and down, and then nodded for her to go on.

"I bought the nicotine in Arizona at a smoke shop and the syringe at a pharmacy in Tennessee. Both are perfectly legal."

"Mom! The lawyer—"

"No." Mel shook her head, and he went quiet. "I asked around when we got here and found out who the caterer for the wedding was. It wasn't hard. It's a small town, and Carol was thrilled about it, bragging to anyone who would listen. Everyone needs staff here. The rest was easy."

"To be clear, you injected a lethal dosage of nicotine into Mr. Clarkson behind his ear," Binder said.

"I did. I hoped it was a lethal amount. Everything I read told me it should be."

"You did it at the end of the cocktail party," I said. "Up on the lawn when he was scanning for a place to sit. I saw him rubbing his hair as he walked to the dining pavilion. I thought an insect had bitten him."

"Yes," Mel said. "That's what I did. Now the state of Maine can take care of me for the rest of my life, since I clearly can't take care of myself. And my son will be free to live his life without the burden of me."

"You aren't a burden." Jordan said it without hope. He knew the time for hope had passed.

"I would have become one in time."

Binder told Mel she'd need to give a formal statement at the police station. I didn't see her story changing.

Jordan was a witness. He'd need to give a statement, too, after his hand was stitched. We all went down to the dock, where the state troopers and a marine patrol boat waited. Our Whaler was back. Sonny had returned to his family.

Tom and I lingered on the dock. He kissed me and held me tight. "You're sure you're okay?" he said. "I have to go.'

"I am and I know."

CHAPTER TWENTY-SIX

Tom called me a month later. We'd talked on the phone every day, but I could tell from the moment I said hello that this call was different.

"Can you come to town between lunch and dinner service? I'm on my way to meet with Zoey. Jamie's on duty. He's talking to the chief to see if he can get off, but it's the middle of summer, and there's no one to take his shift. I'd like you to be there, just in case."

My stomach formed into a tight ball. "Just in case of what?"

"Zoey's DNA results came back today. Just in case she needs you."

"I'll take the *Jacquie II* to town after lunch and meet you outside her place at 3:00. Can you tell me what the results show?"

"That information's confidential," he answered. "If Zoey says it's okay for you to be there, then it's okay."

The summer had been magnificent so far, day after day of the kind of weather that made people say, "This is why we live in Maine." Lunch service had been sold out and flawless, at least as far as any of the guests sitting at the picnic tables could tell. As I walked to the boat, dozens of people told me how much they loved the meal and the island, the boat tour, and the people they'd met along the way. That's why we called it a "dining experience."

I paused to watch Jack, who was running around the great lawn like a loon. When the lunch customers departed, he owned the place until the dinner guests arrived, king of all he surveyed. An island was a wonderful place for a child, a place without cars or school, a place where everyone knew him and watched out for him.

My heart constricted. *This is what I want. Island children, like Livvie and me, like my mother and her mother.*

I had loved spending the summer at Windsholme, where I woke up each morning to the smell of the ocean, the sound of gulls screeching, and my family all around me. The problem was, I was waking up alone.

Watching my nephew, I daydreamed for so long about a future that might never be that Captain George had to blow the *Jacquie II*'s horn a second time to attract my attention. I ran to the dock and up the gangway.

I walked rapidly from the town pier to Lupine Design. In mid-summer, Busman's Harbor's sidewalks were crowded with tourists. "Excuse me, excuse me, excuse me," I called as I strode by. To friends and townspeople who recognized me, I gave a hasty wave.

Tom's unmarked state car was parked in the lot

behind the studio. As I looked down the drive, I saw him climb out. He'd called ahead. Zoey met us both at the door at the back of the building, then hustled us quickly upstairs.

In the last month, she'd popped, her pregnancy going from invisible to unmistakable. I hadn't seen her in that time, and neither had Tom. She must have noticed our surprise because she said, "I know. Baby Dawes." Her arms encircled her belly, she smiled and some of the tension went out of the room.

We sat in her living room. She no longer lived at the apartment. Some of her furniture and a great deal of her artwork had been moved to Jamie's big house right after they'd returned from their honeymoon. As a result, the formerly warm apartment had an abandoned look, as if the tenants had run into the street with whatever they could carry during an apocalyptic event. I hoped we weren't about to witness one.

"Is it okay that I'm here?" I asked her.

"I *want* you here."

"Zoey, as I told you on the phone, we have your DNA results, along with Kendall Clarkson's." Tom leaned forward in his seat on the low couch. Zoey was in the mid-century chair across from us, a slightly higher seat it was easier for her to get in and out of.

All month, I'd been unsure what I wanted the DNA to show. Was it worse to have a father who was a con man and a murder victim, or to have a father you had never met at all? The former, I thought, but I'd had a close and loving relationship with my father, even though I'd lost him young. It wasn't for me to say how Zoey should feel.

"Yes?" She was alert but not alarmed, curious

but not anxious. I marveled at her calm. But then, nothing could change the past, a lesson life had taught Zoey again and again.

"You are not related to Kendall Clarkson," Tom said, "whose real name was Kenneth Clark."

I let out a long breath.

"Oh, I . . ." Zoey groped for words. She was disappointed, that was clear. I moved to the chair next to her and took one of her hands. The other remained cradling Baby Dawes. Zoey swallowed. "What about Amelia? Is she related to him? Are we related to each other?"

Tom cleared his throat. "Amelia Gerhart was not, ultimately, a subject of this investigation. We had no reason to have her DNA analyzed or to examine her relationship to Clark, who is dead. However, if that's something you and Amelia want to pursue on your own, you should certainly do so."

"I see." Zoey shifted in her chair, already uncomfortable with the weight she was bearing. "How did Clark know all those details about how my father and mother fell in love, where they lived, the portraits they painted of each other?"

"There was a close familial match for you in a database," Tom said. I squeezed Zoey's hand, and she squeezed back. "You have a probable parental match with a California inmate named Ezekiel Curran. He died in prison in 2012."

Zoey's face crumpled. I moved to the arm of her chair and took her in my arms. I couldn't see her face, but I felt her tears fall on my bare arm. "I'm sorry," I whispered.

"Clarkson's convictions were mostly for fraud, and stealing—not victimless, but never violent crimes. Zeke Curran, on the other hand, was con-

victed of armed robbery and murder. He robbed a
bank with four other men. The bank manager and
a security guard were killed. In neither case did
Curran pull the trigger, but it was what we call a
'joint enterprise,' which made him as guilty as the
rest.

"Ordinarily, Clark and Curran would have been
kept in very different facilities. But sentenced to
life, Curran turned on his coconspirators and
helped put them and even some of the people
they were beholden to in jail. A part of his deal was
that he would be in a better prison, and he would
never be in one where any of the people he had informed on was housed. As a result, Curran and
Clark spent a year as bunkmates in the same facility. Plenty of time to swap stories."

"Curran," Zoey hesitated. "My dad must have
told Clark my full name. Otherwise, how would
Clark have found me? Which means—" She couldn't
go on, choked with sobs.

"That your dad knew about you," I finished.

Zoey cried for a good long time, while Tom and
I waited. It felt impossible to know what to do or
say. He got her water. I held her and petted her.
Every gesture seemed inadequate.

Eventually, Zoey calmed. "He never left prison,
so he couldn't be Amelia's—" She couldn't go on.

"He may have had conjugal visits," Tom said.
"They'll be a record somewhere if he did."

Zoey nodded. "What did he die of?"

"Lung cancer," Tom handed over a slim folder.
"I don't have much information. He was neither a
suspect nor the victim in this investigation, so we
had no official reason to request more. Since
Curran died in prison, there'll be a record of what

happened with his remains. If they were released to a family member, that might help you track down your relatives."

"Thank you." Zoey sniffed again, but the flood was over.

Hard-soled shoes bounded up the stairs to the apartment. "What's going on?" Jamie burst into the room.

Tom rose from his seat on the couch, and I disentangled myself from Zoey and stood, too.

"Not a match for Clarkson," Tom said briefly, and he gestured Jamie toward Zoey's side. Jamie went to her immediately, taking her in his arms.

"Call me if you have any questions," Tom said to Jamie, who nodded an acknowledgment.

Tom and I went down the stairs, though the retail store, and out to the busy sidewalk. He put an arm around my shoulder and hugged me to his side. "Are you okay?"

I answered the question with a request. "Stay on Morrow Island tonight."

Tom's arm dropped to his side. "I have to be in Paris in the morning."

Paris, Maine, he meant, of course. Still the name made me smile.

He kissed me and murmured, "Sorry," and walked toward his car.

I turned toward the town pier. I'd have to hustle if I was going to catch the *Jacquie II's* dinner trip. Then, out of the corner of my eye, I saw Tom stop and turn abruptly. "The heck with it," he called. "Will you give me a boat ride back to the harbor in the morning?"

"Of course," I said. "With pleasure."

CHAPTER TWENTY-SEVEN

On the Wednesday after Labor Day, the Snowden Family Clambake was closed for the day. The sign at the ticket booth said, "private event."

Fifteen of us gathered for a much different sort of wedding. Jacqueline Snowden married Captain George McQuaig on the great lawn of Windsholme. Livvie and I stood up for Mom, Sonny and Gus for the captain.

George was resplendent in full captain's regalia, including a double-breasted navy jacket, white pants, and a hat with gold braid on the brim. He had trimmed his long white hair and beard for the occasion, though not by much.

Mom was radiant in a dress she had purchased from Stowaway Resortwear, a shop that sold smart clothing to tourists and wealthy summer people. "They had the dress in black. It fit me like a glove and made me feel wonderful. But I couldn't do it. Your father will be enough of a presence on the wedding day without me there in widow's weeds. I was ready to give up when the owner said, 'You have to have that dress.' She went to the brand's website, where she orders clothes for the shop, and there it was in pale green! I can say with certainty I'm the only person in Busman's Harbor who owns this dress."

Mom wasn't wrong that my father would be with us on the wedding day. He was everywhere at the simple ceremony and the luncheon afterward. Not only had he been my mother's husband for thirty-five years, father to Livvie and me, and Captain George's best friend, he had built, rebuilt, or renewed almost everything around us. Not Windsholme, which had burned and been rescued after he died, but everything else on the island. He was with me all day. I didn't wish him away. He had never wanted anything except happiness for my mother.

Mom and George had asked Quentin Tupper to perform the ceremony. He was a friend and the silent partner in the Snowden Family Clambake who had rescued Morrow Island and kept it from leaving our family not once, but twice. Quentin, dressed as always in khaki shorts, nonetheless imbued the ceremony with an appropriate solemnity. The vows were so short even Jack didn't have time to squirm.

"Is it over already?" Mrs. Gus asked, loud enough for everyone in the tiny group to hear.

Vee and Fee shushed her, equally loudly.

To cover up, those of us in the wedding party, almost equal in number to the other guests, burst into applause. Soon everyone was clapping, and we headed to the dining pavilion for a potluck lunch.

I strolled along with Zoey. She was beautiful as

always and fully pregnant, like she'd hidden a beach ball under her colorful summer dress. It had turned out she and Amelia weren't sisters. Amelia's father, a forger, had also shared a cell with Kenneth Clark. In typical Zoey fashion, she decided to ignore this inconvenient fact. Who cared, she asked, about differences in a few chromosomes? She talked Amelia into moving to Maine to learn how to make pottery. Amelia turned out to be both talented and driven, which I appreciated. We would need all hands on deck to cover Zoey's maternity leave.

"I haven't had a chance to show you the proofs from the wedding photographer yet." As she walked, Zoey pulled out her phone and scrolled through the photos. That brought Jamie jogging over to us, just in case. I could tell by his look he would have preferred, given her altered center of gravity, for Zoey to pay attention and keep her eyes ahead. He hovered at her elbow, wise enough not to say anything.

"Here." She handed the phone to me, smiling. "Scroll through to the right."

I looked at the screen, hazy in the sun's glare. I expected a perfect image of a smiling bride and groom, or maybe pictures of Zoey, Livvie, and me, laughing as we dressed for the ceremony. Instead, in a series of images shot frame by frame, I watched the beautiful, five-tiered wedding cake shimmy, wobble, and go over. Bill Lascelle and Derek Quinn were captured underneath, looking up in open-mouthed shock as the bottom layers covered them.

I laughed, scrolled back through the photos, and laughed some more. Zoey joined in. The laughter brought Tom over. There was no profes-

sional photographer today. Mom had asked him to
do the honors with his phone. He'd hung back to
get a few more shots of the bride and groom.
"What's so funny?"

I handed him the phone, and he squinted at the
pictures.

"Funny for you, maybe. You weren't in that pile.
What do you think, Jamie?"

Jamie was already smiling, and then he burst
into laughter. Tom did too, and then we all did.

"I told you we'd laugh about it someday," Zoey
said to me.

"You told me it would be a wedding no one
would ever forget. I think you achieved it."

We'd held twelve more weddings at Windsholme, filling every weekend of our short Maine
summer. I had seen ugly bridesmaids' dresses,
grouchy mothers-in-law-to-be, and inebriated best
men slurring through speeches, and had heard
some seriously poor music choices. But there had
never been a murder, or a melee, or a cake falling
in a perfect arc.

But most of all, I had seen love. Love of one
partner for another. Love of parents for their children and grandchildren. Love of families. Love of
friends. We had worked hard and learned so
much. We were already fully booked for next summer, and I couldn't wait.

Today's wedding meal was spread out across two
picnic tables. There was lobster salad made from
lobsters cooked and cleaned by Sonny and Page,
potato salad made by me, and tomato salad made
by Livvie with tomatoes fresh from her summer
garden. Captain George had baked bread. Fee and
Mrs. Gus had each contributed a pie—one blue-

berry, the other peach. "We'll skip the cake," Mom had said.

Lunch was wonderful, the pies delicious, the last taste of summer. My mother rose and raised her glass. "I never thought I would do this again, but I have been persuaded. If I have learned anything in the past few years, it is this. Grab life. Grab love. Whenever you can."

Was it my imagination, or was she looking straight at Tom when she said it?

Mom and George were leaving on a trip to Montreal and Quebec. When they got back, they'd be living in Mom's house.

The Clambake was winding down for the season. We'd be open for a few more weeks, but only on weekends and only for lunch. Livvie and her family had already moved back to town. Jack was starting second grade, and Page was going to be a senior. The years had flown. Livvie was back at Lupine Design, and by the next week I would be, too.

I was the last one living on Morrow Island, alone except for the cat, Le Roi, who'd stayed to keep me company. I loved the solitude, even the dark, dark nights. Windsholme creaked and groaned as the new parts settled in with the old. I was already sleeping under blankets on the cool evenings. Enough was enough. It was time to go home.

I was as excited to get back to Lupine this fall as I had been to open the Clambake in the spring. The business was solid and expanding. Zoey had an idea of taking advantage of Amelia's and Livvie's skills by developing new lines of painted pottery. She'd had me run the numbers with a profit share for each of them included.

The plan was for me to live in Zoey's apartment over Lupine. It would be a work-live situation. I'd already moved my desk up from my tiny office downstairs. I'd been calculating for months the revenue we'd have to make for me to hire an assistant, and we were on the cusp. Once he or she got there, the apartment would be more office than home. I wasn't worried. I didn't think I'd be living there for long.

Before the guests left, Tom put his phone on a tripod and set the timer, and we all gathered for the official wedding portrait.

I love the photograph. Mom and George, Fee and Vee, Gus and Mrs. Gus, Jamie and Zoey, Livvie, Sonny, Jack, with Le Roi at his feet, Page, Quentin, Tom and me—all sporting goofy grins, linking arms, loving each other.

CHAPTER TWENTY-EIGHT

Five years later

The photo from Mom and George's wedding sits on my mantlepiece now, in my apartment in Windsholme, where we live in the summer. The Snowden Family Clambake lives on, much as it always has, because, as I have come to see, tradition is the point.

Tom lives here, too. It turns out the logistics weren't so complicated. We bought him a motorboat so he could commute and rented a dock at the yacht club, where he keeps his car.

We've expanded our apartment into the bedroom next door to make room for our two little girls, three and two. I'm watching them running and screeching on the great lawn right now. Jack is supposed to be babysitting, but he's chasing them, hands held up like a monster's claws, growling all the while. I supposed that counts as babysitting.

For our wedding, Tom and I had wanted to split the difference between Mom and George's little garden party and Zoey and Jamie's traditional do. But Tom's Rhode Island–based family was enormous, and everybody came. Even the sister-in-law he was formerly engaged to. It turned out she was nice and particularly warm toward me. Her loss had been my gain, so I could afford to be gracious.

Learning from history, we didn't have a wedding cake and instead offered our guests whoopie pies, a staple sweet in Maine. The day turned out to be everything we'd ever hoped. I have a photo of the two of us on the mantel, too. The girls love to look at the wedding album and hear about the time before they were born.

When we're not at Windsholme, we live in Wiscasset, a half an hour from Tom's office and twenty minutes from Lupine Design. Wiscasset is the "Prettiest Village in Maine." At least it says so on the sign on Route 1, though the title is heavily disputed. The logistics came together as soon as Tom and I determined that we had to figure them out.

Lieutenant Binder shocked everyone two years ago by taking a job in private security. He said he was worn out facing death every day at work—not his own, but other people's. Tom had already qualified for the promotion, and he got the job. I am so proud of him. It means he's away from home more nights, summer and winter, but I can get by with help from my friends and family.

Page graduated from college this year. She's moving to New York in the fall to work for a financial company, inspired, she claims by her aunt. Me. Before she goes, she'll spend one last summer working at the Clambake. She's one of our best employees.

Lupine Design is thriving. We signed our first licensing deal for manufacturing this spring. For Zoey, the pottery was very much about getting her hands dirty, but she said, as time went on, leveraging her effort and getting paid for work already done, instead having to create each plate and bowl, became attractive. Livvie and Amelia made the models for the first pieces that will come off the line, and they'll share in the licensing revenue.

Zoey and Jamie's first baby turned out to be a boy. They have a little girl, too, the same age as my younger one. Zoey has a biological family now as well as her found family. The children play together all the time.

Linens and Pantries imploded in spectacular fashion, and Mom got laid off with the rest of the employees. She says she's just as happy. With two new grandchildren, she's content to be retired. The captain often stays overnight in their apartment here in Windsholme and rides in with Tom in the morning to ready the *Jacquie II*.

Quentin met a man in Cannes. I love to say that to him. "You met a *mon* in *Con*," I say. It's meant we see even less of him, which causes me to say, "We can't make a *plon* because you have a *mon* in *Con*," until it drives him crazy. I'm happy for him, even if I miss him.

A friend of a friend told a friend who told Livvie that Chris still lives in Florida. I'm sure he wouldn't have stayed if he hadn't reconciled with at least some of his family. He's married and has a baby girl. I'm happy for him.

Fee and Vee closed the Snuggles Inn last year. Making the beds, doing the shopping, and cooking the breakfasts all got to be too much. They can enjoy their own house now year-round, though often when I visit my mother, I see former guests standing on their front porch, come by to say how much the place meant to them.

Gus died a year ago in March. He finished the lunch rush, took off his apron, and was gone. In the way of long marriages, Mrs. Gus went two months later. Their son and his wife run the restaurant now. They don't have the same attitude about people "from away" that Gus did. Like sane capitalists and business owners, they are happy to serve tourists. But they've kept the menu the same, and in the winter, there are no tourists. I take the girls there because I want the restaurant to be part of their childhoods. But I always get a pang when I look behind the counter and Gus isn't there. He and Mrs. Gus are buried in the Busman's Harbor cemetery, and I often go to see them when I visit my dad.

Which isn't as often as I'd like. Life gets complicated with a preschooler and a toddler, a husband often out of town for work, a full-time job, and a seasonal job. The days are long, but the months fly by. On the days that are hard, when one little girl is screaming in the bathtub and the other is naked and dripping, just outside the door, throwing everything out of the laundry basket, I remind myself of what my mother said on the day of her second wedding. "Grab life. Grab love." And hold on for the ride.

RECIPES

Lobster-Caviar Canapés

In Torn Asunder, *the caterer, Carol Trevett, makes these amazing canapés. In real life, my husband, Bill Carito, developed the recipe. We tested them on a group of Maine mystery authors and their spouses at a potluck dinner, where they were universally acclaimed. "Put them in the book," everyone said.*

Ingredients for the Mushroom Duxelles

2 tablespoons butter, divided
1 tablespoon olive oil
1 pound mushrooms, finely chopped
1 teaspoon herbes de Provence
2 tablespoons heavy cream
Salt and pepper to taste

Ingredients for the Final Preparation

1 package phyllo dough, precooked small tart
    shells, defrosted if frozen
½ pound cooked lobster meat, chopped into
    half-inch pieces, gently warmed in butter
4 ounces crème fraîche
1 to 2 ounces of your favorite caviar
Chopped chives

Instructions for the Duxelles

Melt 1 tablespoon butter and 1 tablespoon oil in a skillet on medium-high heat.

Add mushrooms and cook until they have given up all their liquid and it has evaporated.

Stir in herbes de Provence and cook 1 minute; it's okay if the mushrooms begin to brown a little.

Stir in cream and cook 1 minute more.

Remove from heat and stir in the remaining butter.

Add salt and pepper to taste.

Set aside to cool about 20 minutes.

Instructions for the Final Preparation

Spread the bottom of each shell with the duxelles.

Top with 1 or 2 pieces of warmed lobster followed by a dollop of crème fraîche and $\frac{1}{8}$ to $\frac{1}{4}$ teaspoon caviar. Sprinkle with chives.

Fennel and Orange Salad

This is another recipe by my husband, Bill Carito. He perfected the salad while we were in Key West last winter, and we served it several times to dinner guests with great results. In Torn Asunder, *the salad is served at Jamie and Zoey's wedding because it is a favorite of Jamie's.*

Ingredients for the Salad

2 medium bulbs fennel
6 medium oranges (preferably blood or cara cara)
1 5-ounce bag chopped romaine
1 5-ounce bag arugula
½ cup dried cranberries
½ cup sliced, toasted almonds
½ cup blue cheese

Instructions for the Salad

Quarter the fennel bulbs, remove the core, and slice very thin.

Remove the skin from the oranges, cutting away the white pith. Slice the oranges and quarter the slices.

Put a layer of romaine, a layer of arugula, a layer of fennel, and a layer of oranges in a large salad bowl. Top with cranberries, toasted almonds, and blue cheese.

Add another layer of each and toss with the dressing. We often put the almonds and blue cheese on the side due to allergies and taste preferences.

Ingredients for the Dressing

2 shallots, chopped
1 teaspoon kosher salt (Diamond Crystal)
½ teaspoon freshly ground black pepper
¼ cup orange juice
¼ cup apple cider vinegar
2 tablespoons maple syrup
½ cup olive oil

Instructions for the Dressing

Mix ingredients in a jar. Dress salad to taste.

Baked Stuffed Lobster Tails

There's a lobster recipe in every Maine Clambake Mystery. It seems the least I can do as a Mainer. This is Jamie and Zoey's wedding entrée.

Ingredients

4 lobster tails, fresh or fresh frozen (approximately 8 ounces each)
1 cup panko breadcrumbs
1 lemon, zested and juiced
½ teaspoon salt
¼ teaspoon pepper
½ teaspoon garlic powder
½ teaspoon paprika
8 tablespoons butter, melted

Instructions

Preheat oven to 450 degrees.

Use a sharp kitchen shears to cut down the back of the lobster to the tail, but not through the tail. Use a spoon to separate the lobster meat from the tail, leaving a small flap connected at the back. Reach in and lift the meat up through the cut in the tail; then lay it on top of the shell. Set each tail on a foil-lined sheet pan.

Mix together the crumbs, lemon zest, and seasonings. Stir in lemon juice and 4 tablespoons of the melted butter.

Brush the tails with 2 tablespoons of melted butter. Pile each tail with stuffing.

Cook in preheated oven for 15 minutes. Turn on broiler and broil for 2 minutes, until browned.

Pour remaining 2 tablespoons of melted butter over tails before serving.

Serves 4.

Asparagus-Mushroom Risotto

At Jamie and Zoey's wedding, the lobster tails are served on a bed of asparagus-mushroom risotto. We like it served that way, too.

Ingredients

1 ounce dried mushrooms
4 cups chicken broth
6 tablespoons butter, divided
4 tablespoons olive oil, divided
1 pound mixed fresh mushrooms, chopped
2 large shallots, chopped
2 cloves garlic, chopped
1 tablespoon dried porcini powder
1½ cup arborio rice
¾ cup white wine
1 pound asparagus, trimmed and cut into
  ¾-inch lengths
1 tablespoon tarragon, chopped
2 tablespoons parsley, chopped
1 cup grated Parmesan cheese

Instructions

Boil 2 cups of water in the microwave, about 5 minutes, and pour over the dried mushrooms. Allow to sit for ½ hour. Drain the mushrooms (reserving liquid for another use) and coarsely chop.

Warm the chicken broth in a separate pan.

Heat a large, deep skillet on medium-high heat. Add 2 tablespoons butter and 2 tablespoons oil.

Add the fresh mushrooms and cook until they give up most of their liquid, about 8 minutes.

Add the reconstituted mushrooms and shallots. Cook another 6 minutes.

Add garlic and dried porcini powder, stir, and cook another 3 minutes.

Add 2 tablespoons butter and the remaining oil, and stir in rice.

Cook, stirring constantly until rice is coated and turning translucent.

Add the wine and stir until it is absorbed.

Begin adding broth by ladlefuls, stirring until each is totally absorbed before adding the next. When halfway through, add the asparagus and herbs. When finished stirring in broth, stir the in cheese. Finish by stirring in the remaining butter.

Chocolate-Covered Toffee Squares

In addition to a lobster recipe, every Maine Clambake Mystery contains at least one recipe from the book my grandmother Ethel McKim gave me for Christmas in 1984, only a few months before she died. I usually make these cookies at Christmas, but in Torn Asunder, *I gave them to Jamie and Zoey's wedding guests because I felt badly about them missing out on the cake.*

Ingredients

For the base

1 cup butter
1 cup light brown sugar
1 egg yolk, beaten
1 teaspoon vanilla
2 cups flour
½ teaspoon salt

For the top

12 ounces high-quality chocolate (milk or dark, as you prefer)
1 cup chopped nuts (pecans or walnuts, as you prefer; these can also be left out)

Instructions

Preheat oven to 350 degrees.

Mix cookie ingredients together using a food processor or mixer.

Cover a cookie sheet with parchment paper.

Spread the cookie dough thinly across the parchment paper; it should be about a quarter inch thick.

Bake in preheated oven for 15–20 minutes.

While baking, melt the chocolate in a double boiler.

When the cookies come out of the oven, spread the melted chocolate across the top with a rubber spatula. Sprinkle with the chopped nuts.

Do not cut into squares until the cookies and the chocolate are completely cool. Cut into any size you like.

ACKNOWLEDGMENTS

First, let's address the elephant in the room.

Yes, this is the last Maine Clambake Mystery.

The series began with a wedding and ended with a wedding. This book began with a wedding and ended with a wedding. Symmetry.

If you've been a faithful reader of the novels and novellas from the beginning or you joined us along the way, first of all, I say thank you. You've enabled me to write this series of twelve books and have them published and sent out into the world. You've been gracious when we've met in person or on the Web. You've sent me emails to say how much you loved the books or, with great passion, to let me know about the things you didn't like. I cannot tell you what this has meant to me.

From this writing life, I have gained friends and community and a whole second career I never expected. I will be forever grateful.

The decision to end the series was mine. I have been writing about the Snowden Family Clambake for thirteen wonderful years, and it's time to move on. Besides, the good citizens of Busman's Harbor deserve a break. They've been living in a little town with one of the highest murder rates in the world for over a decade.

Will you see my work in print again? I don't know. I wrote when I hadn't a hope in the world of being published. I don't see why I would stop writing now. The vagaries of the publishing world are such that being lucky once doesn't mean you will be again. I also have other things that are important to me and an ever-increasing awareness that there is limited time to accomplish them. For now, I'll say farewell and not good-bye, and we'll see what develops.

For this book, I would particularly like to thank Luci Zahray, "the Poison Lady," for her help with the weapon in this case. She suggested nicotine fit in my fictional scenario and helped me understand how long it would need to take effect, how the victim would react, and how law-enforcement personnel and the medical examiner might conclude it was the poison used. I did make a lot of things up, however, and Luci isn't responsible for those. If you're a writer, she is a tremendous resource. If you're not a writer, you shouldn't be contacting her. She will not help you kill an actual person.

A special thank you to the Moore family and all the folks at the real, not fictional, Cabbage Island Clambake in Boothbay Harbor, Maine. They have supported me by answering questions, selling the books in their gift shop, and putting up with bodies littered all over their island's fictional counterpart. If you are ever in mid-coast Maine, you should pay them a visit.

Thank you to Bill Lascelle, the high bidder to name a character at the Friends of the Wiscasset Public Library auction. I hope you enjoyed your character's contributions to the mystery. Always support your public library!

Thank you to Jessica Ellicott, who has helped me brainstorm the last several Maine Clambake novels and novellas. She offers coaching services through her website. If you are an author in need, I highly recommend her. Thanks also to author Sherry Harris, who always reads my manuscripts and offers enormously helpful feedback, no matter how late I get them to her.

Thank you to Jen McKee, my virtual assistant. I absolutely could not navigate this writer life without her. (To be clear, Jen is a real person. It's the assistance that takes place across the virtual world.)

Since this is the last book, I want to particularly thank my agent, John Talbot, the first person to utter the word "clambake" at the inception of this series. We've been together for the whole ride, and I am very grateful.

I also want to thank everyone at Kensington Publishing. Every person I have ever dealt with there has been helpful and professional. I particularly want to recognize my editor, John Scognamiglio, who bought and supported the series. Also, my publicist, Larissa Ackerman, who has been incredibly supportive of the series and of me.

I wish also to thank the members of the writing community who have been with me on this journey, many of whom have been acknowledged by name in dedications to the earlier books: my fellow Wicked Authors, the Maine crime-writing community, my original writers group, Sisters in Crime (National and New England), the New England Crime Bake, Grub Street, the Maine Crime Wave, and the Maine Writers and Publishers Alliance. I could not have done it without you. Or I might have done it, but I would never have had so much fun along the way.

As always, to my family. My husband, Bill, has supported every step in this adventure, up to and including developing these recipes. There's no way to return his support in equal measure, so he'll have to settle for "I love you." And to Robert, Sunny, and Viola Carito, and Kate, Luke, Etta, and Sylvie Donius, I cannot say enough. Viola was a babe in arms when the first book was published. None of us had met Luke yet, and Etta and Sylvie weren't even an idea. Yet you have all joined in the merry band. From now on, I hope Gram won't be in the corner typing when we're on vacation. With so much love.